A
Boomer in the Bud

JAMES LAKE

All you need is love.

THE
BEATLES

Chapter One

It all began with an invitation I received on the Monday morning I turned twenty-two. And seeing that I'm a Gemini who was born on the twenty-second of May, all those lucky twos made me think that it must have been fate . . . although of course I know better now.

I'd just pulled on a pair of patched jeans and an old *Rubber Soul* t-shirt, and was about to head into town to meet one of the guys in my band for a late breakfast, when the phone in my trailer's tiny kitchen rang. Now I know what you're thinking: A trailer, for God's sake. How tacky is that? But to tell you the truth it was actually a pretty cool place to live. Not only was it knotty pine inside and out, but it sat all by itself on a heavily wooded two acre lot, and for a small town kid who'd just graduated from college the week before, and had about as much money as he did common sense, the rent was a hell of a deal. Eighty dollars a month. And that wasn't bad back in 67.

Anyway, when I answered the phone I was greeted by a man whose voice I didn't recognize, although he was obviously quite a bit older than me, and quite a bit more refined too. "Hello, Mr. Adamson," he said. "My name's Jonathon Frazier. I'm a lawyer, and literary agent, and I'm calling on behalf of a client, Ellen Harper."

Ellen *Harper*?! The name rendered me mute.

"Mr. Adamson?"

"Yes, I'm here. Sorry. It's just that I'm not used to getting phone calls on behalf of famous authors."

I

"I doubt many people are, Mr. Adamson. Be that as it may, Miss Harper would like to meet with you. She's quite taken with your award-winning story, and wishes to discuss it. Would that be of interest to you?"

Of interest? Of *interest?!* Hell, it was a dream come true. I'd just won a fiction competition sponsored by the writing program at my college, a competition endowed by none other than the aforementioned Ellen Harper, and now she wanted to *meet* with me? Happy birthday indeed.

"Well of course," I told Mr. Frazier. "I'd be honored to meet Miss Harper. You just tell me when and where, and I guarantee that I'll be there."

"Very well then. If you're free, she'd like you to drop by around one o'clock this afternoon. I've been instructed to give you directions."

And that's how, two hours later, I found myself chugging along through the Appalachian foothills of southern Ohio in my beat-up old Volkswagen Beetle—which I'd affectionately named Betsy. She struggled a little going up the steep grades the roads in that area were infamous for, but I'd had her for more than two years by then and she hadn't failed me yet, so I had faith that she'd get me to wherever I was going.

Ellen Harper. I could hardly believe my good fortune. In fact as Betsy putt-putted up an especially long climb, I looked out at a couple of cows grazing in a nearby field and wondered if I might have been hallucinating. After all, Ellen Harper was not only one of the best-selling writers of the twentieth century, but she was also a notorious recluse, a woman who shunned both the literary spotlight and public life in general.

And maybe that's why I was so nervous, my fingers tapping out a steady drumbeat on the steering wheel. Here I was about to meet a woman whose work had influenced me for years, and who would therefore make the best of all possible literary mentors, and I hardly even knew anything about her. I mean, she was born and raised in these hills. I knew that, as well as the fact that she'd moved to New York in the mid 40's to become a writer, and soon put out a wildly successful first novel that made her an instant celebrity. And then of course I knew that she'd just as suddenly dropped out of sight, returning to her beloved homeland and a life of total seclusion. But that's about it. That's all I knew.

Or at least that's all I knew for sure. And I say that because, as is often the case when somebody as compelling as Ellen Harper so suddenly vanishes from the public eye, there were rumors upon rumors that swarmed savagely around her. One was that she'd had a nervous breakdown. Another suggested a stroke. And yet another a tragic accident that had left her terribly disfigured. Most damning of all, however, was the rumor that she'd chosen to hide away from the world to protect her sexual identity. After all, in the twenty years since she'd left New York there'd been nothing to suggest that she'd ever married, or even had a boyfriend for that matter. And therefore people wondered.

To tell you the truth, though, I couldn't have cared less about any of that petty nonsense. The only thing I wanted to find out was whether or not she'd been writing all that time. Seriously. She hadn't published anything since that first novel in 44. *Nothing*. Not a word. *Zip*. Nada. And because of that nobody knew if she'd been turning out any meaningful work or not.

I sure as hell hoped she had, though, because that one novel was simply amazing. Yes indeed, *The Sky's the Limit*, a truly phenomenal read. It tells the story of Miss Harper's fictional alter ego, Eleanor Taylor, a starry-eyed country girl who goes to the big city, takes on the good old boys in the publishing industry, and triumphs against all odds—a book so relentlessly romantic that to me it was downright transcendent. And I mean to tell you, the critics loved it. The reading public loved it. And *everybody* loved Ellen Harper. She was plainspoken, straightforward, and all but aglow with an innocent aura of optimism. So I suppose it's really not all that surprising that she quickly became a beacon of hope to an America just then easing out of the dark days of the Depression and World War II. In fact, between the time of her sudden success and the afternoon that I drove out to meet with her (the rumors swarming around her not-with-standing), she'd been elevated to almost mythical status as a prefeminist heroine, a shining example of the potential of women, the very prototype of those who would follow. Or in other words, a force to be reckoned with.

So you can see why I was more than a little uneasy as I turned off the backwoods road I'd been travelling, and onto a gravel driveway that led me into a forest and around a bend to a formidable iron gate. It was black, and ornate, and anchored in stately stone posts. Rolling down my window, I began to scan the post to my left for a buzzer to push, an intercom to talk into, or any other means of letting somebody know that I'd arrived . . . when from out of nowhere the gate suddenly parted in the middle and slowly started to swing open. I mean, talk about *shocked!* Hidden security cameras may be commonplace now, but they certainly weren't back then. And when you add that to the fact that I was still pretty damn naive, that gate swinging open all by itself seemed nothing short of miraculous—which of course added to what was already, for me, a considerable state of awe.

Therefore I was filled with anticipation as I followed Ellen Harper's gravel driveway ever deeper into the forest, and then up a steady rise. What was I about to find up there, a Tudor mansion? A Colonial estate? Or perhaps even a Medieval castle?

And given those musings, I couldn't help but feel just a little let down when I eventually drove out into a clearing at the top of a really long ridge and pulled up in front of a plain old farmhouse. Granted it was a big one, and it was clearly well maintained, but still it was just a farmhouse nonetheless. White clapboard siding. Dark shutters. And a screened-in wraparound porch.

Making sure to leave Betsy in gear—the emergency brake didn't work any-more—I was just climbing out when the screen door opened to reveal an older gentleman so impeccably dressed that my initial impression was that he might have been a butler. Tall, lean, and almost painfully erect, he had an impressive head of well-groomed gray hair, and a neatly trimmed gray mustache.

"Mr. Adamson, I believe," he said as I came up the steps, extending a slender blue-veined hand that belied the strength of his grip. "As you may have assumed I'm Jonathan Frazier, Miss Harper's agent and, I might add, good friend. She's delighted you could come."

"Well I'm delighted too, Mr. Frazier," I replied. And no sooner had I heard what I said than I knew that I needed to calm down. Relax. Settle into myself. I mean hell, I never used words like "delighted."

But Jonathan Frazier didn't seem to notice. Nodding ever so slightly, he held the door open so that I could come up onto the porch, and then promptly led me around to the back of the house, saying, "Please make yourself comfortable, Mr. Adamson. Miss Harper would like you to feel at home."

4

And with that he gave me a stiff little bow and politely took his leave. At first I just stood there, awkwardly unsure of exactly what I should do. But then I remembered from fighting stage fright as a performer that it helps to get a feel for the venue, so I drew in a deep breath and began to take a look around.

And believe me, I'm not exaggerating when I say that I couldn't have imagined a more perfect place for a writer like Ellen Harper to kick back and hang out in. There was a wooden swing with a neatly folded afghan on the seat, a matching set of Adirondack chairs, and much to my surprise—and dare I say delight?—an acoustic guitar propped up against the back wall. A Martin D-14 no less. On top of that there were healthy green plants everywhere. Potted ferns as tall as I was stood off to both sides. A variety of ivys hung down from the ceiling. And jars full of herbs lined the sill that ran all the way around the outer perimeter.

But it was the view out back that truly sucked the air right out of my lungs. The farmhouse had been built on the very edge of the ridge, and the forest beneath it fell away for at least a mile before opening out into a deep green valley, the stream that ran through its rolling meadows shining silver in the midday light.

Stepping up to the screen to get a better look, I then noticed a series of terraced gardens that had been cut into the hillside, each lush and colorful, and immaculately tended. And I was just beginning to marvel at all the work that must have gone into them when a disembodied female voice said, "Doesn't that get terribly hot in the summer?"

Needless to say that caught me off guard, and all I could manage was a rather lame, "Pardon me?"

"All that hair," the voice said, and I realized then that it was coming from behind the potted fern to my left. "Doesn't it make you uncomfortable at times?"

"Only on the really humid days," I admitted. "But otherwise I hardly even notice it."

"Well that's good to hear, cause I like it. It suits you." And perfectly in tune she softly sang out, "And the tiiimes they are a-chaaanginn."

"You like Dylan?" I wondered, somewhat shocked, but definitely pleased.

"Sure. How could you not like the musical voice of a generation as rebellious as yours? My only regret's that I was born too soon to get in on much of the action. This country's long overdue for a cultural overhaul, and I kinda feel as if I'm missin' out on all the fun."

And I can't even begin to tell you how relieved I was to hear that, because I'd taken a lot of crap from people her age, and had been worried about how she might perceive me. How worried, you might ask? Well, worried enough to change out of my jeans and t-shirt into khakis, a black turtleneck, and pointy-toed Beatles boots. It's what I thought a hip young writer should look like in these post-Kerouac and Ginsberg days. Hell I even considered bringing along a meerschaum pipe, but then decided at the last minute that it would probably be overkill.

"There's no need for you to keep standin' there, you know," Ellen Harper then noted. "You're welcome to pull up a chair."

"Yes ma'am," I said, plopping down into the nearest Adirondack.

"And no need for formality neither," she added with an earthly chuckle. "Most folks around here just call me Ellie."

It was then I became aware that, having sat down, I could see her eyes peering out at me through a slit between two dark green fronds. They were blue, and bright, and full of a lively curiosity—the eyes of a woman clearly enjoying the moment. "So can you do that?" she asked me.

"Do what?" I wondered, so entranced by those eyes that I'd lost my train of thought.

"Call me Ellie."

"I don't know why not," I told her. "If that's what you want."

"Good. Then you won't mind if I call you Andy. Cause the way I see it, Andy, is that you're gonna be gettin' a real good look into my innermost thoughts, so it only makes sense to be on a first-name basis."

"I'm afraid that I don't understand." And I was about to add "Miss Harper," but caught myself.

"Well it's like this, Andy. I'm not one much for small talk, so I'm gonna get right down to it. I know a lotta folks think it's taken me God's own amount of time, but just this past month I finally finished a rough draft of my second novel, and I'd like you to help me whip the manuscript into some sorta shape."

The mere thought seemed so absurd that my gut reaction was to downplay it. "So you want me to be your *typist*?"

Her eyes suddenly sparkled with amusement. "It's actually a bit more complicated than that. I guess you might say that what I'm lookin' for is somethin' along the lines of an editorial assistant."

Editorial *assistant*?! And for the second time in less than an hour I wondered if I might have been hallucinating. I mean, come on. There I was sitting on the back porch of an isolated farmhouse with reclusive author Ellen Harper, and she'd just asked me to assist her in editing the novel the literary world had been anxiously awaiting for more than twenty years. It simply didn't seem real. And maybe that's why I boldly decided to test my luck. "Why me?" I asked her.

And she was quick to respond. "Because of why I had Jonathan invite you out here, Andy. Plain and simple. I really liked your story. And by that I mean not just the storyline itself, but the gently poetic style as well. How you ever thought to write about a young David Henry Thoreau awakening to the world of nature, I don't know. But it's a brilliant idea, and you pulled it off beautifully. And since so much of my new novel focuses on a similar theme, I just figured you'd have a darn good feel for what it is I'm tryin' to say. That's all."

And what did I do then? Did I rise to the occasion, accepting the offer of a lifetime with a confidence-inspiring blend of grace, and humility, and enthusiasm? Well . . . not exactly. I'm still kind of embarrassed to admit it, but I was so overwhelmed that all I could do was mutter one of the many mindless platitudes of the day. "Oh wow," I said, so at a loss for words that a few seconds later I repeated myself.

"You'll have to help me out there," Ellen Harper then told me with another earthly chuckle. "Is that a yes or a no?"

"Oh by all means a *yes*," I blurted out, nearly coming up off of my chair. "A most *definite* yes. In fact I can't think of *anything* I'd rather do . . . although I have to say that I'm somewhat confused. I mean, why not just edit the novel yourself?"

And for reasons I wouldn't be aware of for months that question clearly stunned her. Drawing back an inch or two, she lapsed into a thoughtful silence, and her eyes underwent a subtle change. They were still bright on the surface, alive with the spirit of the moment, but beneath that veneer there appeared an . . . I wasn't sure, a longing, or a sadness of some sort, something deep-seated but vague. And whatever it might have been was reflected in her voice when she eventually said, "Let's just say that I'm tired, Andy. I'm tired of being by myself, and I'm tired of working alone. Can't we just leave it at that for now?"

Fine by me. In fact I was *more* than happy to leave it at that, because I could tell by the way the blood drained out of her cheeks that confiding in me had been hard on her. We did keep talking for another twenty minutes or so, though, initially scheduling a work date—one o'clock the following afternoon—and then just getting to know each other a little. She took a truly genuine interest in me too. I felt that as deeply at the time as I know it for certain now. Asking question after insightful question, she charmed me into opening up about my childhood, and school years, and dreams for the future. It was almost as if she believed that in order to grant me access to her inner-most thoughts she'd first have to develop an intimate understanding of who *I* really was inside.

But in spite of Ellen Harper's obvious desire to get to know me, it soon became apparent that she wouldn't be able to continue much longer. She was simply too fatigued. I could see it in her eyes, which had become hazy, and heavy-lidded, and appeared to periodically drift out of focus. And I could hear it in her voice, which had grown softer, and weaker, and more tentative. It even got to the point where I was thinking that it would be downright rude of me not to excuse myself . . . when the door behind me opened and Jonathan Frazier reappeared.

"I'm afraid you'll have to be going now," he said as I stood, and I was a bit taken aback at how somber he sounded. "Miss Harper needs to rest."

And it was then that I noticed, sticking out from behind the base of the potted fern shielding Ellen Harper, the corner of a colorful quilt. "And don't forget," she practically whispered then. "One o'clock tomorrow afternoon."

"Not to worry," I assured her. "I'll be here, and I'll be ready to get right to work too. You can count on me."

And smiling over at an unsmiling Jonathan Frazier, I nodded to let him know that I was ready to leave, and he dutifully escorted me back around the house and out onto the front lawn, the screen door squeaking softly as it swung shut behind me.

Chapter Two

"She wants you to *what?*" my girlfriend Nicki asked, and I could tell by the exasperation in her voice that she didn't really care for the idea.

"Help edit her new novel," I repeated.

"But I thought you were going to graduate school."

"I am, Nick, but classes don't start until September, you know. And that gives me the whole summer to work with."

She just stood there staring at me for a moment, her hands on her hips—and then crinkled her nose, a sure sign of displeasure. "At least I hope she pays well."

"Hard to say. We never got around to discussing that."

Rolling her eyes and releasing a sigh, she spun away and began to unpack the sack of groceries she'd set on my kitchen counter. "That is soooo like you," she said. "Mr. Romantic. Mr. Carefree. Mr. Everything's Going to be Fine."

"Listen Nicki," I told her, taking her lightly by the shoulders and turning her gently back towards me. She was wearing knee socks, a plaid skirt, and a white blouse with a prim little Peter Pan collar, her lips pursed in a half-hearted pout. And in spite of being angry she looked as cute as could be. "This is a great opportunity for me, and chances are I'll never get another one like it. If I *really* want to be a writer, and you know that I do, I pretty much have to take it."

All the fight went out of her at that. Putting down the loaf of garlic bread she held, she leaned in and lay her head on my chest, her auburn hair freshly washed and smelling of honeysuckle. "But I *worry* about that, Andy. I have from the start. It's a tough way for anybody to make a living."

"Not tonight, okay? It's my birthday. Let's just have a nice dinner, and we can talk about it later. And in the meantime I'll try to be more practical. When I see Miss Harper tomorrow I'll ask her about the money part, and tell her that I can only work until school starts. How's that?"

Pulling back, she gave me a smile and a quick peck on the cheek. Then she returned to unpacking the groceries. So I went back to what I'd been doing before she arrived, tuning the Rickenbacker 12-string the drummer in my band had found for me at a trade show a few days earlier. It was used, but in great shape. A real beauty. And I wanted to try it out at practice that night.

"Oh," and Nicki said a few minutes later, not bothering to look up from the meatballs she was browning. "Mom and Dad want us to come up for brunch on Saturday. Is that okay with you? I'd be happy to drive."

And I knew why too. Nicki's parents were nice enough and all, but they were from an extremely well-to-do Columbus suburb, and *very* image conscious, so they didn't like having Betsy parked in front of their house. Hell, for that matter it had taken them a long time to even warm up to me, and not just because of my jeans and long hair either. It had to do with a lot of different things. For one I was pretty much a country boy, and therefore not up to their high social standards. And for another I was a Protestant while they were devout Catholics (and even worse I'd stopped going to church altogether a few years before). But more than anything else they were uneasy about Nicki dating me simply because I was adopted, which in those days still carried a pretty nasty social stigma, especially when you consider her family's strong Irish roots, her mother a Delany and her father an O'Grady. It made them nervous about the prospect of grandchildren. I don't mean to be overly hard on them, though. At heart they were really good people. We just didn't have a whole lot in common.

"So do you want to go?" Nicki prompted.

"Yeah, sure," I said. "It's all right with me." Not that I really had any choice.

"Good. Cause dad said he had a graduation present for you, and he sounded kind of excited about it."

"That's nice of him," I told her. And having settled the matter we then sat down to a good solid meal of spaghetti and meatballs, a staple among the college crowd. It was plentiful, tasty, and cheap. And it truly did turn out to be a nice dinner too. Nicki was scheduled to attend an Inter-Sorority Council meeting at seven—she was a Pi Phi—so she told me about some of the issues they'd be addressing, and as always she was so sincere, and so dedicated to doing what she believed to be in everyone's best interest, that I couldn't help but be supportive. Then I told her about a new song I was writing, and she made me promise to let her hear it as soon as it was finished. And finally as I was clearing the dishes she went over to her shoulder bag on the couch and came back with a rectangular white box that had a blue bow taped to the top. It was the perfect size to hold a tie.

"Happy birthday," she said. "I sure hope you like it."

Now you've got to keep in mind, I don't even wear a tie now, much less back in my scruffy semi-hippie days, so it wasn't exactly easy for me to work up any enthusiasm. Still, I knew that Nicki would've put a lot of thought, and heart, into selecting what she felt was just the right one, so I feigned excitement as I opened the box . . .

Only to find, not a boring old tie at all, but a burnished leather guitar strap with my band's name, Willow Creek, stenciled across the back.

"I thought maybe you'd need it for your new 12-string," she explained with a smile.

Which of course caused me to pretty much melt all over. "Oh Nick," I said, taking her into my arms. "It's beautiful. Thank you so much. I'll definitely wear it at practice tonight."

And as she then joined me in doing the dishes—I washed, she dried—I couldn't help but think about how happy I was that we were still together. I mean, we'd first started dating more than a year and a half before, when I was a junior and she was a freshman. At the time I too was involved in Greek life on campus—Sigma Chi—and she was a Pi Phi pledge. Since then, however, I'd drifted off into the counter-culture and undergone many changes (both inside *and* out), whereas she'd pretty much stayed the same. And yet somehow, and some way, being together still worked—much to the disbelief of many of our friends, some of whom had begun to lose faith in us as a couple as soon as I started playing in a band. We didn't care, though, because we were absolutely certain that our bond was deep enough to withstand anything. So as far as we were concerned the naysayers could all go screw themselves. It was Nicki and Andy against the world. Nicki and Andy forever.

☆ ☆ ☆

Pulling into the dirt lot outside *The Hayloft*, the club my band played in every Saturday night, I left Betsy in gear, got out, and walked around front to unwind the wire that held the hood down (the latch having rusted out over the winter). Then I reached in and took out my new guitar, anxious to finally hear what it sounded like plugged into my big Vox amp.

From the street the place wasn't much to look at, just a concrete block foundation with red brick walls, but the interior was seriously cool. Having been built of the wood salvaged from a 19th century barn, it was all post and beam and rough-hewn paneling. And for a final touch the owner had brought in the old twenty-foot tin feeding trough and installed it in the men's room as the urinal. It was quite the conversation piece too, and it wasn't at all uncommon to belly up to relieve yourself only to have to listen to some drunken yokel on down the line mooing like a contented cow.

Nobody else was there yet, and since the club was closed on Sunday and Monday it was dark and quiet inside. So I turned on all the lights and began to get the equipment up and running. I wasn't really all that good with the soundboard—we left that up to the bass player's girlfriend, an electronic whiz kid—but I did know enough to turn it on and get power to my amp. And I'd just returned to the stage and picked up my guitar when our drummer walked in: Ritchie Starkey, a bantam rooster of a guy. He was only five-six or so, but sinewy, and toned, with a spiky mod haircut that made him appear a hell of a lot taller than he really was. He was also incredibly energetic, always in motion, a veritable whirlwind in concert. I mean, he could lay down the beat for hours on end and seemingly never get tired.

"Any news?" I asked him.

And he just shook his head. "Nope. I'm still on hold. You know my dad, though. He wouldn't have told me he had it covered if he didn't."

I sure hoped so. Like way too many of us back in those days, Ritchie was sweating out the draft. He'd dropped out of college to start a record store, and was therefore I-A, prime for the plucking. So he was doing his best to avoid being called up by Uncle Sam and shipped to Vietnam by trying to get into the National Guard. The problem was that his chances were pretty damn slim, because so many other desperate young men were trying to get in too. Luckily his dad was a high-powered businessman who had a lot of government contacts, and he was calling in all the old favors he could.

Ritchie didn't really want to talk about it, though. I could tell by the way that he changed the subject. "Nice guitar," he said with a grin.

"Thanks to you. And I still can't believe you came up with one just like Jim McGuinn's, same blond finish and everything."

"I'll bet it really rings."

"We're about to find out," I told him, plugging it in and playing a power chord, the room instantly coming alive with the sound of what might have been electrified chimes.

☆ ☆ ☆

"Do you think it needs more treble?" I shouted out from the stage. "The high notes sound a little thin."

"Not from here they don't," Maureen Boyd shouted back. "Come here and I'll show you."

So I took off my guitar, propped it up in its stand, and joined her behind the soundboard at the back of the room. And as soon as she hit "playback" I knew that she was right. The balance was perfect. My new 12-string sounded great.

"See," she said, smiling brightly as always.

And it was all I could do not to give her a hug. Of course that was nothing new, because she was just the huggable type, of average height and pleasantly plump, with curly red hair, sparkling green eyes, and the sweetest chubby cheeks you've ever seen. Plus she had on one of those loose-fitting hippie chick dresses, and as she'd bounced around earlier checking the mix I could tell that she wasn't wearing much of anything else . . . an added incentive if ever there was. I behaved myself, though—not that Maureen would've minded. She was a *very* affectionate woman, and yet innocently so, for she had an Earth Mother spirit. Touching others came easily and naturally to her, as did nurturing, and soothing, and healing. The band was lucky to have her around. She was a constant source of positive energy, a truly luminous presence.

"Keep backing. Keep backing. Keep backing. Keep backing."

"I *am* backing," I said, "but you're pushing too hard. Slow down a little, will you?"

"Sorry," our bass player mumbled.

Not that it was really his fault. He simply didn't know his own strength. His given name was Christopher, Christopher Hillman, but everybody called him "Little John," after the character in *Robin Hood*, because he was . . . well, anything *but* little. A burly bear of a man, he stood over six-five and weighed more than three hundred pounds. And since we were loading a heavy amp into the band's equipment van, and I was walking backwards up a pretty slick ramp, it was all I could do to keep from being knocked on my butt. Not to mention that I kept losing my grip, while Little John was having no trouble holding on to his end.

"How's that?" he asked, having slackened the pace.

"Much better," I told him. And after a nerve-wracking slip or two on my part, we finally finished wrestling the amp into place and stood there panting side by side.

"Thanks for the help," Little John said between breaths, peering down at me intently, his eyes deepset beneath a heavy brow. And given that he also had a wild head of dark hair, a thick full beard, and a decidedly serious demeanor, I could see why more than a few people found him intimidating.

And yet as the old adage goes, looks can be deceiving, and that was certainly the case when it came to Little John. Seriously, you couldn't have asked for a more gentle and sensitive soul. He was a Philosophy and pre-Divinity major, an extremely deep, soft-spoken, and pensive fellow. I couldn't imagine him ever hurting anybody. On the contrary, he was opposed to violence in any form, a pacifist in the truest sense of the word.

"So what do you think about Friday?" he asked as we headed back down the ramp, which bowed heavily under his every step. "Are you with me?"

"Absolutely," I assured him. "But what about Michael? You know that he doesn't like to play for free."

"I was hoping maybe you'd talk to him."

Hearing what might have been the amp shifting, I hopped down into the parking lot and glanced back at the van, which was actually an old Wonder Bread truck, the iconic logo still faintly visible on the side. Everything looked to be okay, though. "I'm certainly willing to give it a try," I told him, "although I can't make any promises. It's ultimately up to him."

"I know," Little John said, lumbering on ahead, his massive shoulders rolling up into a shrug. "And yet something tells me you'll find a way. Somehow you always do."

Oh swell, I thought, the "can't-miss" jinx. Bad karma if ever there was.

✠ ✠ ✠

"A *peace* rally?" Michael Taylor blurted. "Come on, man, not again. We did one just last month."

"Yeah, I know, but this one's supposed to have a really huge turnout, so there'll be a lot of press coverage. And that basically means free publicity. So even though we don't get paid it could still turn out to be a pretty good deal."

I slid down off my bar stool, walked around behind the bar to the cooler, and reached in for a bottle of Little King's ale. "Want another one?"

"Sure," Michael replied, as I fully expected. Out of all the guys in the band, he was by far the heaviest drinker. "How many's that?"

"Two for me, four for you. And don't forget Maureen's glass of wine."

"Got it," he said, grabbing a pen and a cocktail napkin off a tray at the waitress station. We were on the honor system with *The Hayloft's* owner, helping ourselves to whatever we wanted, but keeping a tab and settling up later.

"Besides," I continued as I returned to my seat, sliding a can of Colt 45. over in front of him. "It means added exposure too. Think of all the kids that'll be there who've never seen us before. And if they like what they hear—"

"Jesus Christ, man," Michael said. "We get capacity crowds in here every Saturday as it is. What in the hell are we gonna do if even *more* people show up?"

He had a point there. Not only did we pack the place every week, but we were starting to build a solid regional following too. In fact we'd sold out gigs as far away as Wheeling, and Columbus, and Pittsburgh. And that was clearly on Michael's mind.

"I'll tell you what," he said. "I'll agree to play that rally if you agree to put more time into the band."

Oh no, I thought, here we go again. It had been a conflict between us ever since we'd put together our first band in high school, The Dante's, covering everything from late 50's bobbysocks hits to the supposedly suggestive Kingsmen classic, "Louie-Louie." Michael was bound and determined to do whatever it took to make a career out of performing, while to me it was merely a means to an end. I wanted to get an education and become a writer, not live the grueling day to day grind of a touring musician.

But it wasn't just that. Even our approach to the band was different. For me it was all about the music. I couldn't have cared less about anything else. But for Michael it was all about being a rock star. I mean, he was our leonine stud, lean and athletic, with the perfect head of sandy hair, cheekbones even a male model would envy, and piercing blue eyes that drove female fans into fits of idol worship. And oh how he loved to play the part too, prowling the stage seductively, his voice pulsing with the promise of passion and romance. All of which, in my eyes, was more or less an insult to my musical muse.

What really complicated things, though, was the fact that we were a team, the very definition of "synergy," our whole being greater than the sum of its parts. I played rhythm. He played lead. We shared lead vocals and harmonies. And together we had the power to blow people away.

But more than anything else, I knew that deep in his gut Michael was worried about my commitment to the band simply because I was the primary songwriter. Ritchie and Little John might have contributed the occasional tune, and we did throw a few covers into every concert, but otherwise I was the source of all our material. So Michael knew that, at least for now, he needed me for the band to survive.

But back to the moment. A white lie was in order, or at least an indirect reply. "Well you know how excited I am about my new guitar, "I said. "How could I *not* be inspired to play as much as possible?"

He took a sip of Colt 45. and eyed me suspiciously. And then just as we'd been doing for the past five or six years, we simply put the matter on hold.

Chaper Three

I was out in the yard putting seed in the birdfeeder the next morning when a dark blue Cadillac turned onto the lot, an odd sight in the rugged hills of southern Ohio, where the local folks mostly drove pickups. And it was even stranger still when the Cadillac then pulled up right alongside Betsy and Jonathan Frazier got out, dressed every bit as impeccably as the day before, his grey hair shining softly in the gentle early light.

"Good day, Mr. Adamson," he said as he approached, setting the leather briefcase he carried down onto the grass so that he could shake my hand. "I'm sorry to disturb you, but it's imperative that we speak, and I wanted to do so in person."

"In that case come on in," I told him, having heard something in his voice that made me a little uneasy. "I've got a pot of tea on the stove, and it'll only take me a minute to heat it back up."

"That's very kind of you," he said as he picked up his brief case and followed me inside, looking just about as out of place as anyone ever could. I mean, in a neatly tailored three-piece suit and dress shoes polished to a really high shine, he should have been standing in some Broadway theater, or a five-star restaurant or something, and not in the living room of a jacked-up old trailer full of secondhand furniture.

"Why don't we just sit here at the kitchen table," I told him, turning the burner on under the teapot and clearing away my writing materials. I'd been working on a new short story. "Would you care for milk and sugar? I'm pretty sure I don't have any cream."

"Just the tea will be fine, thank you," Jonathan Frazier said, laying his brief-case on the Formica tabletop and pulling out one of the mismatched dining room chairs. He was the very picture of composure too, sitting there with his hands politely folded in his lap as I got two ceramic mugs down out of the cup-board, filled them with tea, and set one on the plastic placemat in front of him.

No sooner had I too sat down, however, than he took a long and searching look into my eyes, and a heavy air of sadness seemed to settle over him. Releasing a barely audible sigh, he gave me a strangely wistful smile and opened his mouth to speak—but the words got caught in his throat. So he took a moment to collect himself, and then his eyes misted over and he said, "It is with great regret that I have come here to inform you that Miss Harper has passed away."

And that obviously came as a hell of a shock. In fact I was so stunned that at first I didn't even react, and then when I did it was in disbelief. "But that can't be," I told him. "We spoke just yesterday afternoon."

He steadied himself, squaring his shoulders, and then assured me that, in-deed, her heart had simply given out overnight. "It was all very sudden," he added. "She'd been in failing health for some time now, but no one ever ex-pected—" He had to pause to collect himself again. "But no one ever expected this. She'd been too full of life recently, in great part because she was so happy to have finally finished her new novel."

"I am so sorry," I told him, totally at a loss as to what to say after that.

And we therefore lapsed into an extended silence. It wasn't really an awkward silence, though. Not in the least. It was more like what I guess I'd call a shared moment of grief, for in that instant I honestly did find myself overwhelmed by emotion, although I couldn't have said why. After all, I'd only just met the lady.

"Believe me," Jonathan Frazier said then. "I'm sorry too. And yet I must say that her final days were good ones. Not only had she at long last completed her new novel, but she was greatly looking forward to working with you. 'Just *think* of all that youthful energy,' she told me just the other day. It was exactly what she'd felt she needed."

He slowly bowed his head at that point, staring absently down at the table. So I gave him a moment to be alone with his thoughts before clearing my throat and saying, "Well if it's any consolation, Mr. Frazier, I was looking forward to working with her too. She seemed like a really nice lady, and it was an honor to have been chosen to help her with her manuscript."

That appeared to lift his spirits a bit. Looking back up, he smoothed his trim grey mustache and said, "You are absolutely right, young man. She was indeed a wonderful woman, and I shall miss her terribly. I loved her as I would my own daughter. But as for her manuscript, make no mistake about the fact that I am still counting on you to edit it as she'd wished. It was her dream to see it published, and to fail to make that happen would be an unthinkable disservice to her memory."

And how did I respond to that startling news? Well, in keeping with the standard I'd set so far, I once again went numb. I mean, *me* edit Ellen Harper's new novel? Where would I even begin? How long would it take? And what was I going to tell Nicki? The whole idea made me weak at the knees.

Jonathan Frazier, however, was undaunted. In fact his desire to see Miss Harper's novel published had clearly given him a boost. "The truth of the matter is, Mr. Adamson, that in addition to being Miss Harper's lawyer, and agent, I am also the executor of her literary estate. And in that capacity I am prepared to make you a generous offer. Beyond having you help edit her new novel, she had also planned to ask you to assist her in organizing her other writings, of which there are many. She'd been quite prolific all these years, turning out a great deal of work on a variety of subjects. For example, she spent much of her time exploring the mystery of the creative process, and there are copious notes to that effect scattered throughout her library."

He broke off for a moment to reach across the table, open his briefcase, and draw out a small stack of index cards. "By way of background, about all I am able to tell you is that her personal approach to writing was highly organic. She wrote in overlapping cycles, always doubling back to revise what she'd previously written before moving ahead each day, so that each piece essentially grew out of itself. And with that in mind I've brought along these few notes for you to consider, simply to give you some insight into the way in which she worked."

Handing me the index cards, he then returned to his briefcase and drew out a number of official-looking documents. "What I have here is a contract," he continued. "It stipulates your editorial and organizational duties, for which you are to be paid ten thousand dollars as a retainer against five percent of whatever royalties Miss Harper's new book may earn. And just by way of comparison, *The Sky's the Limit* still generates more than two hundred thousand a year in royalties, so even though there are no guarantees, the amount you will make over time is likely to be considerable."

Ten thousand dollars against five percent of the royalties? Two hundred thousand a year? Hell, for a kid who was lucky to pull down a couple hundred a month playing in a band, those figures were so mindboggling that they sent my brain into overload.

And Jonathan Frazier must have seen that. "There's no need for you to decide at the moment," he said, gently sliding the contract my way. "Take a few days. Read this over carefully. And let me know by the first of the week. I have yet to make the news of Miss Harper's death public, but once I do there will no doubt be the usual crush of media attention. Given the fickle nature of our so-called 'pop' culture, however, I expect it to be relatively brief, especially due to the fact that, as directed in her will, Miss Harper has already been cremated and there are no current plans for a memorial service. Therefore I believe it would be safe to assume that the reporters will be gone by next Monday and, should you choose to take on this project, you will be able to begin work then. Do you have any immediate questions?"

Questions? Sure, I had a lot of questions, one of which was, "What in the hell's going on here?" I mean, I'd just graduated from college, for God's sake, and was in no way prepared for life to suddenly come rushing at me like a runaway train. I needed a chance to step back, take a deep breath, and sort things out. First things first, however. There was at least one practical matter that simply had to be addressed.

"I know it'd be hard to say," I told him, "but do you have any idea how long this might take? And the reason I ask is that I'm supposed to start graduate school in the fall."

He took a moment to consider that concern, and then said, "To be perfectly frank, Mr. Adamson, in my estimation it's highly unlikely that you would be able to complete the project in a matter of mere months. Having said that, however, I must add that I also see no reason why we couldn't work around your schedule once classes do begin. That is, if that would be satisfactory to you."

And how could I possibly argue with that? I mean, the guy was bending over backwards to accommodate me. Still, even though I was acutely aware that most young writers would sell their soul to be given a break like this, I wasn't at all convinced that I was truly the man for the job. Did I *really* have the ability to do justice to Miss Harper's new novel? I was, after all, pretty much still a novice. And what about the rest of her work? Would I even be able to understand it? Nope, I wasn't feeling all that confident about any of this. In fact the only thing I knew for certain was that if I *did* sign that contract, the world as I knew it would soon be coming to an end.

☆ ☆ ☆

The rest of the morning passed by in a blur. I kinda remember whipping up a mushroom and Swiss cheese omelet, and then wandering outside with my Gibson acoustic to play a few songs about sorrow and loss. Other than that, though, I think I more or less just poked around. There was simply too much going on in my overburdened young mind for me to concentrate on any one thing.

In the early afternoon, however, I finally found a focal point. It was an absolutely gorgeous day, seventy-five and sunny, the sky a bright blue from one ridge top to the next. So I grabbed the index cards Jonathan Frazier had given me and went out to the little stream behind my trailer—Willow Creek, the inspiration for the name of my band—to sit on the bank and see what Miss Harper had to say about the creative process.

And take my word for it, I no sooner read through her notes than I knew I'd be willing to do whatever it took to bring every last bit of her writing to life. I mean, those notes spoke to me as if they were my own, for they expressed ideas I'd already vaguely thought of, but had never been able to put into words. Some of her observations were purely practical, little bits of advice about the actual craft of writing, such as, "*Every detail must have meaning.*

If it doesn't further the plot, develop a character, or enhance a setting, then why bother with it at all?" And, *"Critical to your momentum: Always leave off with either notes or rough copy that will lead you straight into your next day's work."*

But it was the more profound insights that truly spoke to the heart of me, the words of wisdom about the miracle of creativity itself, such as, *"All writing originates at the hourglass point at which inspiration flows into consciousness."* And, *"Writing must be an exhalation, a means of rejoicing in the spirit of life within you."*

And I don't mean to be overly dramatic about this, but as I finished reading Ellen Harper's thoughts I got the strangest feeling that they'd been written down just for me. I'm telling you, my entire *being* suddenly started to reverberate. And I realized then as I never had before that I had indeed somehow stumbled onto my one true calling. It wasn't going to be easy. I had no illusions about that, because the odds of my success were incredibly slim, and I'd have to sacrifice a lot in my personal life to even stand a chance. But sitting there on the bank that day I really didn't give a damn. All I knew was that, as surely as there were butterflies drifting along on the wind currents above Willow Creek, I was in the grip of some unknown force that was trying real hard to sweep me on into my future, and I'd be a fool not to abandon myself to it. No matter what challenges might lie before me, I was now fully aware that I had no other choice but to suck it up and do what I'd been destined to do all along. Oh I'd *thought* about it, and I'd *talked* about it, but I'd never really known it deep inside until that very moment. Come what may, I was going to be a writer.

✶ ✶ ✶

With a little over an hour of light left in the sky, I laced up my Adidas and went out for a run—an uncommonly long one for me. Granted, I pretty much ran everyday, but usually no more than a mile or two. On that evening, however, I ran almost seven. That's how wired I was.

It was a nice time of night to be working out too, the light breeze in the valley having turned cool and dry. Heading out onto the abandoned Jeep road that paralled Willow Creek, I loped along slowly until my legs loosened up and I really found my stride. And then I picked up the pace, but not too much, since I wasn't in any real hurry. In fact given everything I'd been through in the past day and a half, I knew the longer that I stayed out the better.

At first I wasn't able to quiet my mind. It skipped around as whimsically as if I were dreaming, from memories of Ellen Harper's eyes, and the colorful quilt at her feet, to worries about the commitment to writing I'd made that afternoon. Eventually, however, as always when I ran through those hills, I slowly drifted off into the world of nature: the wind rustling the leaves in the shadowy trees, and the murmur of the water on its journey to the sea. And then thankfully, and mercifully, I knew only the sound of the air rushing in and out of my lungs. And in and out of my lungs. And in and out of my lungs.

And then I knew nothing at all.

✶ ✶ ✶

The dawn sun streamed in through my bathroom window as I stared into the mirror above the little round sink. It reminded me of when I was twelve years old, and still reeling from the shock of being told I was adopted. I'd stared at my reflection a lot in those days, scrutinizing my features in a futile attempt to determine where it was that I might have come from. Blond hair, blue eyes, and really fair skin, I was pretty sure that I was some sort of a Scandinavian and/or western European blend. But what kind of a blend? That's what I didn't know. Was I Swedish? English? Danish? German? A good part of me was convinced that I'd *never* find out, since the mother and father I'd always known and loved simply didn't have a clue. The whole process of adoption was hush-hush at the time, and the only information they'd been given was that my birth parents had chosen to remain anonymous. Everything else had been wiped off the record.

And that's why I spent hours in front of the mirror as a kid, gazing deeply into my own troubled young eyes and wondering who that was looking back at me in wonder. It felt oddly as if some stranger's life had suddenly taken over my own, a disturbing thought that weighed heavily upon me until my junior year in high school. At that point, as fate would have it, I happened upon a line in *Moby Dick* that completely changed my outlook. It appears in the scene where Ishmael decides the hell with all the trauma surrounding the hunt for the great white whale, he's simply going to embrace "a genial sort of desperado philosophy" to see him through the many tough times ahead.

And that sounded good to me. In fact, there was a carefree quality about Ishmael's attitude that I thought would suit me just fine. Yes indeed, I could easily see myself back then as a genial desperado.

And you know, as I stepped away from the bathroom mirror on that morning in 67, I couldn't help but grin, because I realized that I still looked at myself in pretty much the same way. Gangly and a bit gawky at a slender six-two, with jaw-length blond hair and *really* straight bangs (alá Brian Jones of The Rolling Stones, or the kid on the Dutch Boy paint can), I was happy enough just being me, regardless of the nature of the blood coursing through my veins. All things considered, I'd kinda grown to like the mystery of not knowing who I was. I mean, it made me unique, truly one of a kind. And I couldn't think of anything wrong with that.

☆ ☆ ☆

After cleaning up and throwing on jean shorts and a faded Monterey Pop t-shirt, I headed out to the kitchen to brew a pot of tea, stopping in the living room just long enough to turn on my old hand-me-down Motorola, a black and white console no less. The sky out front had grown so dark that I wanted to get a weather forecast.

And even though I have to confess that I should have been expecting what happened next, the truth of the matter is that it caught me completely by surprise. That's how naive I could be in those days. Instead of a weatherman, it was Hugh Downs of the *Today* show who slowly faded into view. Of course that was no big deal. He was on almost every weekday morning. It was what he was saying that stopped me dead in my tracks.

"And the mystery of Miss Harper's death merely underscores the many questions surrounding the life she led over the past twenty years," he intoned ever so sincerely. And then he went on to recite the litany of rumors that had hounded Ellen Harper from the time that she first went into seclusion. The breakdown. The disfigurement. Even the suspicions about her sexual identity. With his unblinking eyes staring straight into the camera, and his carefully measured voice just as steady as could be, Hugh Downs detailed every last bit of pseudo-drama that decency and time would allow. And then the screen cut to a shot of a young Barbara Walters. She was standing in front of the imposing iron gate at the entrance to Miss Harper's property, where at least a dozen other talking heads were jockeying for position.

And that's when I realized that I didn't really care to be exposed to anymore of that gossipy crap. I'd only met Ellen Harper that one lone time, and so I'd never had the chance to get to know her very well. But I was willing to bet pretty much anything that her last twenty years hadn't been at all like what was just then being suggested on national TV.

Flipping off the Motorola, I promised myself I'd avoid watching and/or reading anything the media had to say over the next couple of days. That way I could form my own opinion of Ellen Harper based solely on the two sources I had personal access to. One, Jonathan Frazier. And two, whatever I happened to uncover in her library. In other words, I didn't want the sensationalized innuendos of a ratings-based news program to distort my point of view. On the contrary, I suddenly found that I had a burning desire to get to know Ellen Harper on my own.

Chapter Four

Maureen had just finished running the band through its final sound check when our host for the afternoon—Alan Snyder, a local poet and political activist—stepped up onto the flatbed truck that was serving as our make-shift stage. It sat right in the middle of a meadow on Alan's small farm just outside of town, home to the first ever Southern Ohio Festival of Peace and Love. And from what I could tell by looking out over the sea of humanity that stretched out in front of me, it was going to be a rousing success. Not only was the concert venue packed, but the dozen or so jewelry, clothing, and food booths in the back were doing a really brisk business—as was the Joni Mitchell-like blond in the flowered dress who was painting butterflies on people's cheeks for free.

"Are you boys about ready to go then?" Alan asked, looking every bit the counter-culture icon in his little round glasses, brown ponytail, and peace sym-bol t-shirt—not to mention the embroidered jeans.

"We're all set," I told him.

"In that case I'll open things up by saying a few words, and then as soon as I'm done I'll introduce you. Okay?"

And with that he walked up to the center mike, tapped it to make sure that it was on, and launched into what turned out to be a twenty minute inspi-rational talk about practical ways to work together to create a more peaceful existence. It was a beautiful presentation too, brimming over with the idealism that came to characterize the 60's. As volunteers wandered through the crowd handing out colorful pamphlets full of supporting information, he spoke in the lyrical voice that only a poet can, stressing the need for religious tolerance, racial unity, and gender equality. And then he made an impassioned plea, imploring his youthful listeners to channel their growing resistance to the Vietnam war into creative expressions of non-violent protest. And all the while his audience was spellbound. You could see it in the rapt attention in their faces, and in the stillness with which they sat.

Until, that is, with a final flourish of poetic insight Alan Snyder intoned an ancient Native American affirmation: "As I harmonize with nature and all living beings, I breathe life into the spirit of peace." Then he quickly spun around to give us an encouraging grin, and swinging back to the mike he concluded by saying, "And now all you future leaders of the free world, let us join hands and share in the joyful music of our favorite hometown troubadours, the Willow . . . Creek . . . *BAND!*"

And as the starry-eyed masses eagerly answered his call, reaching out to one another to form an unbroken human chain, we burst into the opening bars of a song we'd been working on ever since I first decided that I simply had to have an electric 12-string, "Turn, Turn, Turn," a verse from *Ecclesiastes* set to music by Pete Seeger and popularized by the Byrds. Then we followed that up with another pastoral Byrd's tune, "The Bells of Rhymney." And we closed out our set by doing extended jam versions of two of my originals, "Today," a song about the beauty of living in the moment, and "Renaissance Fair," which details a magical morning in the life of a young English lad who's in the midst of coming of age. They were typical of what I wrote back then, not angry songs about cultural rebellion and needless wars nobody could win, but uplifting songs about the miracle of human potential. After all, it was a time of innocence, and not just for me, but for my entire generation. We believed in possibility. The power of *now*. The ability to change the world. And that's why on that lovely May afternoon, the sun shining down upon me and my heart full of hope, I threw my head back and I sang.

✹ ✹ ✹

"I see Julie's here," Nicki said matter-of-factly, although she couldn't fool me. I knew how she felt.

"That's out of my hands," I told her.

"I know, but that doesn't mean that I have to like it."

We were killing time between sets by sitting on the front edge of the flatbed truck and looking out over the crowd, and she'd just spotted an old girlfriend of mine, Julie Marshall, a willowy art major I'd dated my freshman year. As I recall, however, the relationship had only lasted for a month or two, because she'd proven to be a bit too spacy, and far too needy, for me. You know, the kind who almost immediately gets it into her head that you're soul mates, and then clings and clings and won't let go. And even though I did everything in my power to let her down gently, all that did was make her desperate. I'm serious. You name it, she did it. The lovesick letters. The frantic phone calls. Even a night spent in her car in front of my dorm when I refused to come out and talk to her. Over time, however, she'd slowly lost heart, and eventually left me alone.

Or at least, she'd left me alone until Michael and I formed Willow Creek, at which point she once again became a nuisance, an omnipresent groupie if you will. I'm not exaggerating either. Wherever we went, she went. I didn't really mind all that much, though, because she was actually a pretty nice person, and mostly kept a respectful distance. It was Nicki who didn't like to have her hanging around, primarily due to the fact that she always hovered right in front of the stage, her adoring eyes fixed directly upon me. I mean, sure it could be unnerving at times, but for the most part I'd grown so used to her that I hardly ever noticed. She was just kind of there, like the mikes, and the amps, and the electrical cords. Unless, that is, Nicki drew her to my attention.

"See anybody else you know?" I wondered, thinking it best to change the subject.

"Sure," she said. "Lots of people. What about you?"

"A bunch of the regulars from the club are here, and of course Michael's 'femme de jour'."

Nicki just giggled, her palms pressed to the wooden truck bed and her legs swinging lazily back and forth. It was a frequent joke between us, because in spite of all his rock star posturing Michael had a fragile ego, and if he didn't have a woman constantly fawning all over him he tended to be insecure. The thing is, it never took him long to become bored with whichever one he happened to be seeing at the moment, so he'd heartlessly dump her and quickly move on to the next. Hence the term "femme de jour," which our drummer Ritchie Starkey had come up with, since Michael's women came and went so fast that Ritchie could never even remember their names. Or as Ritchie himself once so perfectly put it, "He goes through those poor girls like they're guitar picks." And as I think back about it now, I suppose Nicki and I were being insensitive for finding that so funny, although for some reason we did. Perhaps we were simply too young and immature to appreciate the pain he was causing.

"Hey," Nicki said then. "Guess who else I just saw?"

"Who's that?"

"Dicky Haldeman."

And we both had to laugh about that, because Dicky had been a source of humor around town for quite a while by then. He was a Criminal Justice doctoral student who passed himself off as a tree-hugging hippie who'd totally rejected the so-called "straight" world. I mean he had it all, the long hair, the bellbottoms, the sandals, even the "groovy" and "far-out, man" lingo. And what's so funny about that? I'll tell you: Everybody and his mother knew that the butthead was actually a plant, an undercover police informant. That's how paranoid the government was becoming, and it's also what was so comical, because Dicky had no idea that his cover had been blown, and so it was really easy for people to mess with him. For example, one practical joker I knew sidled up to Dicky at an anti-war rally and tried to coerce him into sharing a joint—but only so that he could watch Dickey squirm as he tried to worm his way out of it. And then later in the day when that same joker was busted—surprise, surprise—the "marijuana" he had on him turned out to be oregano. Everybody got a good laugh out of that one.

And as long as I'm on the subject of humor, I feel compelled to mention one other guy who attended our concert that lovely spring day, Jerry Hayden, an outspoken radical and newly elected president of the local SDS chapter. Of course that in itself isn't all that funny. But what *is* funny (at least to me anyway), is that by the mid-80's he'd morphed into a Reaganite Republican, a diehard conservative if ever there was. The epitome of the Establishment man. Now *that's* funny!

But I digress, so back to those first heady days of my 23rd year. And I have to confess, as Nicki and I sat up there on that makeshift stage, my arm draped loosely around her waist and her head laying gently on my shoulder, I wasn't really all that concerned about who happened to be in the audience. Honestly, I was more than content just being with Nicki, and being in love, and being on the verge of what I just knew was going to turn out to be a life-changing literary adventure. In fact the hundreds of people then spread out before me ultimately seemed so inconsequential that they might as well have not even been there at all.

"Now remember," Nicki said as I drove Betsy down her parent's tree-lined street. "Don't mention anything about Miss Harper's new novel. And I have a really good reason for saying that too, Andy. I just can't tell you what it is yet. Okay?"

"If that's what you want," I replied. "Although you will let me know at some point, right?"

"Believe me," she said confidently. "I won't have to. You'll figure it out on your own."

I merely smiled, and then turned my attention to the row of stately houses we were passing, mostly Colonials, and French Provincials, and the occasional stone mansion, each sitting in the midst of a perfectly manicured lawn. Upper Covington was one of the two wealthiest suburbs in Columbus at the time, predominantly WASP with a smattering of Catholics, and clear across town from Drexel Heights, its heavily Jewish counterpart—no minorities need apply. And the cars along the curb reflected all the money to be found there too. There were Cadillacs, and Lincolns, and Mercedes galore, even a high-priced muscle car or two. In fact, pulling up in front of the O'Grady family's sprawling Tudor, I parked right behind a silver Corvette Stingray, its surface so highly polished that I had to shield my eyes from the glare.

"Betsy doesn't quite fit in here, does she?" I noted as we got out and headed up the freshly sealed asphalt driveway. It was my way of making light of the fact that Nicki's parents were embarrassed to have her dating someone who owned such a beat-up old car. Not that I really cared. In fact I'd insisted on driving. It was a point of pride with me.

"Well here's the happy couple now," Nicki's dad Patrick said as we passed through the ivy-covered trellis that led to a beautifully landscaped back patio and pool. Disengaging himself from the knot of nattily dressed 40-somethings he'd been chatting with, he set aside the Bloody Mary he held and stepped up to give his daughter a hug. Then he turned to me and shook my hand. "Happy birthday there, Andy. Twenty-two and newly graduated, eh? You couldn't ask for a better time of life."

"Thanks Mr. O'Grady. I have to admit that it does feel pretty good."

"And now on to graduate school, I hear," he added jovially, looking quite sporty in his dark crew cut, white polo, and plaid Bermuda shorts. As Nicki had told me on the drive up, he was entertaining a client for the day, and the brunch was merely a quick stopover between golf at the country club and choice seats at the Ohio State spring football game. As the senior partner in a third-generation corporate law firm, he was expected to keep the big money rolling in. And I have to give the man credit, he was damn good at it too.

Eileen O'Grady appeared at my side then, as cool and resplendent as always. In a cream-colored sundress that set off both her slender figure and perfect tan, and her blond hair done up in a stylish French twist, she was a 60's version of what's now referred to as a "trophy wife". Not that Mr. O'Grady didn't love her, because it was obvious that he did. But it was just as obvious that he took great pride in showing her off as well.

"I'm so glad you could come, Andy" she said, laying a hand lightly on my arm. "We haven't seen you in awhile."

"I know," I told her. "It's been a busy couple of months, what with the band, and writing, and final exams and all."

She gave me a neutral smile, clearly not very interested in any of those subjects. Then she wrapped an arm around Nicki's shoulder and led her off into the house, saying something vague about the need for a little "girl talk".

"Women," Mr. O'Grady said once they were gone, absently shaking his head. "There's simply no understanding them, is there my boy?"

I knew better than to get drawn into a conversation like that, though, so I steered it in another direction. "How'd you do this morning?" I asked him.

"Pretty good. Low 80's. And I'd have to say that's right on track for this early in the season. It's a shame you don't play, though. I'd like nothing better than to take you over to the club and give you a solid thrashing." And to emphasize that he was only kidding he slapped me on the back. It was his way of showing that he accepted me as "one of the guys".

Little did he know that it didn't go over very well. And neither did what he had to say next. "So, you still driving that old junk-bucket?"

"Yes sir, I am. It's been a real good car to me."

"Well just so you know, one of my partners has a brother who owns a Ford dealership, and I'm sure he'd be happy to cut you a deal. Just say the word and I'll set up an appointment."

"Thank you," I told him with a shallow nod. "I'll definitely keep that in mind."

"You do that, my boy. I'd be glad to help out. Now if you'll excuse me I have guests to see to. Feel free to get something to eat, and I'll talk to you again in a bit. I have a little surprise in store I think you're going to enjoy."

I nodded again as he grinned and walked away, and then I wandered on over to the catering station, which consisted of a long linen-covered table full of chafing dishes, fine china, and sterling silverware, and then a shorter linen-covered table full of wine and liquor bottles. Behind each one stood a young black girl in a white shirt, white pants, and a red bow tie.

"May I get you something, sir," the one tending bar inquired as I approached. And since it was far too early in the day for me to start drinking—it would only make me sleepy—I asked her if she had any lemonade.

"Yes sir," she said, reaching beneath the table and drawing out a porcelain pitcher. "Would you care for crushed ice with that?"

"Cubes'll do just fine, thanks."

And as she then smiled and picked up a pair of silver ice tongs, I glanced over to check out the buffet. It was quite the spread too. There were breakfast foods such as Eggs Benedict and omelets, and dinner foods such as Beef Stroganoff and noodles, with a wide variety of other choices in-between. And I was just trying to decide what I was in the mood for when I received another slap on the back, and a booming voice behind me said, "Way to go there, Andy. Patrick tells me they broke down and gave you a degree after all."

Oh no, I thought. Please no. Not Willie Hanover. He was one of Mr. O'Grady's boyhood buddies, a filthy rich insurance broker who to this day remains one of the loudest and most obnoxious people I've ever met. It was almost as if he believed that having so much money entitled him to act like a jackass half the time. I knew what he was getting at too, so I reminded myself to keep my composure as I turned around to face him, a portly man with a florid face and rapidly thinning hair. And as usual he was dressed to draw attention to himself, in this case in a bright red Hawaiian shirt with a topless hula dancer on the front.

"Hey Mr. Hanover," I said. "And you're right. They decided I wasn't as big a threat to national security as they'd feared."

"I'm anxious to hear the whole story," he said heartily. "From what little I've been told, it sounds like it must be a doozy."

No doubt about that. It was a doozy indeed . . . although typical of the times. Less than a month before I was set to graduate, my professor in a Public Speaking class had assigned us the task of coming up with a highly dramatic way to open a presentation. For example, one guy began by taking off his pants, and then spoke about how to iron them. Another walked over to the window and punched out a pane, and then demonstrated how to replace it. And so on.

I, on the other hand, had a slightly more radical idea in mind. I gave a speech condemning the draft that began with me burning my draft card. Or at least that's what my audience thought, much to the unbridled delight of some, and the absolute disgust of others. What they didn't know, however, was that I'd actually burned a Xerox copy. My real draft card was tucked safely away in my wallet.

Unfortunately my professor didn't know that either, and after class she called me into her office, closed the door, and lectured the hell out of me for having the nerve to use her classroom as a political platform. Then she told me quite bluntly that she'd turned me in to campus security.

And the retribution I suffered was swift, although relatively painless. The very next day I was ordered to attend a hearing before the head of campus security and an FBI agent who'd been brought in from Cleveland. And I've gotta tell you, in spite of the cold-hearted manner in which 60's bureaucrats are most often characterized, they both turned out to be perfectly decent men. After allowing me to explain my actions, they checked to see that I did indeed still have my real draft card, and then patiently informed me that it was illegal to copy it and I could have been fined ten thousand dollars and sent to prison for three years. However, due to my spotless record and high academic standing they'd chosen not to prosecute. And that was that.

Except, of course, for the slightly more lengthy university review to determine whether or not my transgression had been severe enough to warrant my expulsion. And that's what Willie Hanover had been referring to, because I'd sweated out the verdict until the week of graduation before being told that in the administration's estimation I was still worthy of being awarded a degree. So I gave Mr. Hanover a condensed version of that entire story, and he seemed to get a chuckle out of it.

"Well how about *that?*" he said with a toothy grin. "You kids sure do have the government on edge these days, don't you? It's almost as if they think you're capable of a massive uprising or something."

"Oh, I don't think we'd go *that* far, Mr. Hanover. Or at least I wouldn't anyway. I was just giving a speech. Not that I'm in favor of the draft, mind you, because I'm not—especially when it comes to Vietnam. It's just that I'm not what you'd call an agitator. In my opinion there are better ways to bring about change."

"I'm sure there are, Andy," Mr. Hanover told me with yet another slap on the back. "I'm sure there are. So tell me, now that you're out of college I'll bet you're thinking about your future. And as long as I have you here I'd like to let you now about a new policy we've designed precisely for a young man like yourself."

Luckily Nicki and her folks reappeared at that moment to spirit me away, but not before Willie Hanover was able to force his business card on me. And the irony is, I slipped it into my wallet right on top of my draft card, hoping against hope that I'd never find myself in the unfortunate position of having to use either one.

✳ ✳ ✳

"Now don't forget," Patrick O'Grady said. "This is just for your birthday. I have something a bit more substantial in mind as a graduation present."

We were standing by the deep end of the kidney-shaped pool, right alongside the diving board, me holding the miniature treasure chest I'd just been handed, and Nicki and her parents hovering in anticipation. Thanking them for thinking of me, I opened the lid to find an expensive gold tie-pin and cufflink set, a tiny 24K stamped neatly on each piece. The thing is, as you may recall, I'm not one to dress up all that much, so that set was about as useful to me as a pair of burlap boxers. And yet I knew they meant well, for in their minds they were only doing what they could do to groom me for success in the professional world, and I was sincerely grateful for that.

"I hardly know what to say," I told them, with a special emphasis to Mrs. O'Grady, because in those days shopping was solely the woman's responsibility, so I knew she'd selected the gift. "Thank you so much. The workmanship is beautiful."

She gave me a demure smile, and then a kiss on the cheek. "Happy birthday, Andy," she said, raising a glass of sparkling wine. "And here's wishing you many more."

"I second that," Mr. O'Grady chimed in, raising his Bloody Mary. "Many more indeed. And now ladies," he then said, bowing ever so slightly. "If you'd be so kind as to take your leave, we men have a little business to attend to."

Nicki and her mother exchanged a knowing glance, and then Mrs. O'Grady said that she'd just been thinking about indulging in a bit of dessert anyway, and off they went to the catering station—at which point Mr. O'Grady waved over a man I'd never seen before. He was a good-looking guy too, somewhere in his mid-to-late 30s, with a full head of brown hair and a muscular build. And like a lot of the highly successful men I'd met through the O'Grady's, he had a gleam in his eye that bordered on arrogance.

"So you think Woody's gonna let Otis run wild today, men?" he said as he approached. "Or will he save him for the upcoming season?"

"Don't you worry," Mr. O'Grady replied. "He'll have that boy pounding the defensive line like an automated battering ram. And speaking of the game, we'd better get going in twenty minutes or so. Will that give you enough time to work with?"

"Plenty," his friend said, brushing an ash off the shoulder of the navy sweater vest he wore. He was smoking a fat cigar.

"In that case allow me to introduce you boys. Andy, this is my neighbor Robert Lawson, of the esteemed ad firm Lawson and Finch. And Robert, this is the young man I've been bragging about, Andy Adamson, a recent honors graduate of Ohio Southern."

And having brought the two of us together, Mr. O'Grady then gracefully stepped aside, saying that he had to go round up the rest of the Ohio State fans.

"So," Robert Lawson said once we were alone. "Patrick tells me you're an award-winning writer."

"Yes, sir. I won a fiction competition at school."

"And I understand you're also a songwriter," he added, taking a long pull on his fat cigar and peering out at me through the smoke.

It was then that I got my first inkling of where this conversation might be headed. "Yes, sir," I said again. "And I also write the occasional poem, although I don't really consider myself a poet."

"You know," Robert Lawson told me, his eyes momentarily drifting away. "I wrote a few poems in college myself, mostly sonnets to a sexy little redhead I was dating."

Ah yes, I thought, a shared intimacy. The classic technique for breaking the ice.

And it certainly appeared as if I was right about that too, for Mr. Lawson then segued straight to the point. "Yep," he said. "I sure did enjoy writing those poems. And you know what that says to me, Andy? It says that we're both lucky, in that very few people have a true gift for language, and in my field it's a precious commodity. Which, by the way, is exactly why Patrick felt that you and I should talk. My firm has an internship open this summer, and he thought perhaps the position would help to prepare you for the rigors of graduate school. And who knows, if you're really as good as he keeps telling me you are, we might just have to try to tempt you away from academia, and into the profession. It's a lucrative field, Andy, and with the television market growing by leaps and bounds the future looks even brighter. So what do you think? Can I count on you to showcase your talents at Lawson and Finch?"

I happened to glance down as I considered that offer, chancing upon my reflection in the pool and seeing that I wore a rather pained expression. Of course that's not overly surprising, given that I was thinking about how miserable the young F. Scott Fitzgerald had been after taking a position at a national ad firm in Manhattan, where all he could envision was an endless future of writing such mindless drivel as, "We keep you clean in Abilene."

But I wasn't about to let Robert Lawson know that. It would have been far too rude a response. Besides, I couldn't just flat out say no anyway, since Mr. O'Grady might have taken that as a personal insult.

So looking back up what I said was, "That's extremely kind of you, Mr. Lawson. It sounds like a great opportunity. Unfortunately I'm already in discussions about some editorial work, so I can't really commit to you at the moment. Could you by any chance give me a couple of days?"

Robert Lawson took another long pull on his cigar and nodded empathetically. "Certainly Andy," he said, "but we need to fill the position by the first of the month, so I'll have to know by then."

"I appreciate that, Mr. Lawson," I told him, now fully aware of why Nicki hadn't wanted me to say anything about Miss Harper's new novel. That job offer was her father's graduation gift to me, and she didn't want to see him disappointed before he'd even had the chance to spring the surprise. And besides, I would have been lying to myself if I didn't admit that somewhere deep down inside she too was no doubt hoping I'd take it. Unlike me, she was a very practical person, and often spoke about future considerations like having a family, and a nice house, and all that (which of course meant that we'd need a steady income). So I knew that my dedication to writing was a constant source of concern for her. And I'd like to take a moment here to thank her too, because she rarely if ever nagged me about it. On the contrary, when something was troubling her she tended to patiently and openly speak her mind. And I'll always love her for that.

But back to the brunch. Just after Robert Lawson had excused himself to go join the other men heading off to watch the Buckeyes, a woman I'd always gotten a kick out of took the opportunity to come up and say hello. Her name was Melody Hanover, Willie's wife, and even though I'd seen her play the suburban social games with every bit as much finesse as the very best of them, she was the only one of the O'Grady's friends who'd ever let me know that she also saw right through all the bullshit that involved. A brassy little bottle-blond, she was all designer labels and diamonds. And yet there was just a hint of sleaze about her too. Perhaps it was the obvious boob job, or the unnaturally puffy lips. And then again, it might have been the fact that she was uncommonly free with her affections.

"Well hi there, Andy," she said as she walked up, sliding an arm around my waist and pinching me on the butt. "How's the new college grad?"

"I'm feeling just fine, Mrs. Hanover," I told her. "It's kinda nice to get a break from school."

"So what now, rock stardom?"

I had to smile at that, because the last time Willow Creek had played in Columbus she'd dragged her husband to the gig, and I could tell by the way she ended up dancing in the aisles that she'd really gotten into the music. "To tell you the truth," I said, "you sound just like our lead guitar player. He *really* wants me to commit to the band. I don't know, though. I just don't think I'd enjoy that life, mainly because I'd hate being on the road all the time. So as of right now I'm leaning more towards graduate school."

"Well pooh on you," she said playfully. "And here I was giving some serious thought to becoming a middle-aged groupie."

I knew she was only kidding around, even after she'd reached over to pinch my butt again. But as she smiled up at me through heavily mascaraed eyes, her absolutely stunning cleavage practically popping out of the tight tank-top she wore, I couldn't keep from thinking that there really were a lot of lost souls in their forties who still followed the bands around—although not as many as there were burned-out musicians that age. And briefly picturing myself on stage after twenty-some years of touring, what I saw was a rather pathetic shell of a man struggling desperately to hold onto his rapidly fading youth. And I certainly didn't want to end up like that. So instead of dwelling on such a sobering thought, I took Mrs. Hanover by the arm and led her over to the bar, having decided that it just might be a good time for a cold beer or two after all.

Chapter Five

Having already given me the keys to Ellen Harper's farmhouse, as well as a lesson in how to operate what I found to be an incredibly complicated security system, Jonathan Frazier then handed me a rectangular plastic device. "It's a remote for the front gate," he explained. "You keep it in your car."

And that came as such a complete surprise that I just stood there with my mouth agape. I mean, I wasn't a *total* rube. I had seen a couple of TV remotes— which as strange as it may seem were still an oddity in those days—but I'd certainly never seen a remote that opened a massive iron gate. In fact I hadn't even known the technology existed (except of course in James Bond movies). So needless to say, even though I'd only been at Miss Harper's for a little over an hour, and hadn't even ventured beyond the living room yet, I was already feeling somewhat overwhelmed, and once again began to wonder if I really had what it took to handle this job. Not that I could possibly back out now, since I'd already signed and returned Mr. Frazier's contract.

"And again, I regret having to leave you so soon," he was saying, slipping into a trim grey suit coat, "but I have pressing business back in New York, and it's imperative that I see to it personally. If all goes well, however, I should be able to return by the end of next week. And you have my private number, so if by any chance you find that you do need me, please don't hesitate to call."

"Believe me, I won't," I told him, thinking that I'd no doubt have a thousand and one questions by the time he made it down off the ridge.

"Very well then," he said with a dignified smile, reaching into the interior pocket of his coat and drawing out a leather checkbook. "It's high time that I paid you the first installment of your retainer. I trust a thousand dollars will suffice?"

A thousand *dollars!*? Hell, I could live halfway through the fall on that. And yet I did my best to contain my excitement, since I felt like I'd already been coming across as a bit of a bumpkin, and didn't want to reinforce that image. "Certainly," I told him in my most self-assured voice. "A thousand dollars will do just fine."

"And I'd like to wish you the very best of luck too, Andy," he added as he bent over a wooden end table to write out the check. Then he straightened back up and presented it to me, his eyes misting over just as they had when he'd first told me about Miss Harper's death. "It's an honorable task you've taken on, young man, and I have great faith in your ability to see it all the way through to a successful conclusion."

"Thanks, Mr. Frazier. I'll work really hard. I promise."

"I know you will, Andy," he said, clapping a wrinkled hand on my shoulder. "Miss Harper was absolutely certain that you're just the person to look after her literary affairs, and I never once knew her instincts to fail her."

And just like that he gave me a nod and was gone, out the front door and across the porch, and there I stood, alone in Ellen Harper's living room, so unsure as to what to do next that it was as if I'd gone into paralytic shock or something. Sooner or later I'd have to make my way upstairs to the library. I knew that. But I just wasn't quite ready to confront the many mysteries that awaited me there. Perhaps it had something to do with what Jonathan Frazier had told me when I'd first arrived that morning. Apologizing for not escorting me up to the library himself, he'd explained that it offered such an intimate reflection of Miss Harper, not just as a writer, but as a woman as well, that he hadn't been able to bring himself to enter it since the day that she died.

"You will therefore find it exactly as she left it," he told me. And for some reason that struck me as both deeply touching and yet intimidating as all hell. So as I said, I simply couldn't work up the nerve to go up there yet, and therefore had no idea just what my next move should be.

But then my eye fell on something I'd noticed earlier. There was a state-of-the-art stereo system along the front wall, and on each side of it stood a glassed-in cabinet full of albums. And that's when it dawned on me that I could ease the pressure of entering Miss Harper's library by first learning a little about her through her taste in music.

Unfortunately that plan didn't work out nearly as well as I'd thought, because she ended up having such an eclectic collection of records that the more I looked through it the more elusive she became. I'm serious. As I flipped from album to album I ran across everything from Beethoven to Billy Holliday, and Bob Wills to the Beatles. In fact I couldn't even *think* of a musical genre that wasn't somehow represented there. I mean, the woman just plain loved music. All *kinds* of music. And I didn't know quite what to make of that.

Looking around the rest of the room didn't tell me a whole lot either, and neither did wandering into the kitchen. I mean, it was a farmhouse, and she was a country girl. That was obvious in everything from the rustic furnishings to the cast iron skillet on the stove. Beyond that, though, her home was decidedly nondescript.

And it was then I suddenly knew that I wasn't going to get anywhere at all until I quit procrastinating and hauled my skinny butt upstairs to take on what I now fully believed would be the single greatest challenge of my entire life: Immersing myself in the creative world of Ellen Harper, and by doing so somehow discovering what it meant to truly be a writer.

The first thing that caught my attention was that you entered the library through this really cool opening in the floor, coming up off the top step of a narrow stairwell and straight into the middle of a room so huge that it took up the entire second story of the house. And I was even more pleasantly surprised when I then noticed the enormous amount of light pouring in, for even though the walls behind and off to the sides of me were lined with built-in bookshelves, the one in front of me certainly wasn't. In fact it wasn't even really a wall. It was a massive bay window that faced directly into the sun. On top of that there were four big skylights overhead, one in every quadrant of the sharply angled ceiling. And therefore the entire place was amazingly bright and cheerful. I might even go so far as to say luminous, since it reminded me of being in a solarium.

And the *view!* Oh my god. It was incredible, even more so from the upstairs than it had been from the back porch. With the land sloping down off the ridge and out into a distant valley, it was like looking at a panorama of a nature preserve or something. And that's not just my imagination running wild again either. I mean, there weren't any roads, or any buildings, or even any telephone lines—only forested hills, and rolling meadows, and a stream that sparkled in the early light as it ran through the heart of it all.

In fact it was such a breathtaking scene that I gazed out upon it for quite a while before turning away to explore the contents of Miss Harper's desk, a simple but elegant oak table. It sat right in the middle of the big bay window, with neatly stacked papers and notebooks covering nearly every square inch, and a single matching hardback chair pulled up to the center edge. All in all it was an impressive workplace, the kind that a budding young writer like myself could only dream of ever having. So spellbound was I, in fact, that I briefly drifted off into a fantasy of myself hunched over that desk, pen in hand and bathed in sunlight, the words pouring out of me so feverishly that it was all I could do just to get them down onto the page fast enough.

At some point, however, I eased back into the moment and started to take a more detailed look around, my eyes instantly drawn to the many photographs scattered throughout the room. Quite a few captured natural settings as stunning as the view out back, and yet others featured people and places that held no meaning for me at all.

But it was the pictures of Ellen Harper herself that truly captivated me, and the impact they had was both immediate and profound—for they offered an intimate look into her adult life that shot the hell out of most of the ugly rumors that had hounded her for so long. A breakdown? Not likely. A stroke? No way. Disfigurement? Out of the question. Quite the opposite in fact. Each and every last image showed a radiant woman, tall and slender and in real good shape, with short blond hair, broad cheekbones, and uncommonly bright blue eyes. In what must have been the earliest shot—she looked to barely be into her twenties—she was standing in front of the Statue of Liberty in dark pants and a waist-length jacket, her hands on her hips and a great big smile on her pretty young face. In another she was slightly older, and on horseback, holding the reins as casually as if she'd been riding her entire life. And in a third she was even older still (and yet every bit as vibrant), sitting on a boulder among snow-capped mountains, so aglow with an aura of unbridled joy that she might have just summited Everest.

But my favorite picture was the one that I spotted next to a copper jar on the bookshelf to my right. It revealed a truly mature Ellen Harper, maybe even as old as forty, her face now much fuller and her body having thickened. She was on her knees in the dirt among tomato vines, in overalls, work gloves, and a big straw hat—and the light in her eyes as she looked up at the camera was downright beatific. How a woman could derive so much pleasure from simply working in her garden, I didn't know, but it was sure as hell clear that she did.

And yet as compelling as the pictures of Miss Harper were, I couldn't spend the entire day just standing around gawking at them. There were other elements of her library to consider as well, among them the many artifacts and keepsakes on display. I mean, talk about revealing! For even though each one was totally unique unto itself, as a whole they all touched upon a similar theme: Ellen Harper's love of nature. I'm telling you, I felt as if I'd wandered into a Natural History Museum or something, seeing that I was surrounded by pine cones, and dried flowers, and amazingly colorful crystals. Not to mention the many Native American relics she'd amassed, such as eagle feathers, and gourd rattles, and a flute carved out of a beautifully weathered antler. But more than anything else, Ellen Harper had decorated her library with objects tossed up by the sea, a veritable cornucopia of conch shells, and sand dollars, and stones tumbled smooth by the ever-pounding surf . . . prime examples of the rich bounty this earth has to offer.

And no sooner had I been struck by that sense of natural abundance than I found myself drawn back over to Miss Harper's sun-kissed desk, where a notebook lay directly in front of her chair, perhaps the final one she'd written in before so suddenly passing away. Picking it up, I looked down at the title on the cover and broke into a smile, for what it said so simply and yet eloquently was,

Musings on Mother Earth. And that seemed entirely too perfect to me at the time, entirely too perfect indeed.

And it was then that I had a flash of intuition that was to guide me in my work throughout the whole of that fateful summer, and far, far beyond—because I suddenly knew why I'd been so attracted to Ellen Harper's first novel, and she to my award-winning story. It was all so very simple really. Both of us wrote about the spiritual connection between all living beings and nature. In fact at that moment it occurred to me that the *main* reason I put the pen to the page was to communicate that bond. And now that I think back about it, I'm a little surprised that it had taken me so long to actually come to that conclusion, for ever since my first college English class I'd been devoted to the work of a literary society that had altered the course of American letters by celebrating that bond, the irrepressible romantics now known as the Transcendentalists. Seriously. The mystical insights in their writing had influenced me so powerfully that a few years before I'd even undergone a religious conversion, abandoning the Episcopal faith in which I was raised to follow a deeper and more passionate calling, as yet still somewhat vague and undefined, but undeniable nonetheless—because it stirred my very soul. And I'm not just saying that for dramatic effect either. It's absolutely true. From the moment I was first exposed to the Transcendental worldview I began to question the teachings of the Church, and long for a theology of my own making, one inspired by the essays and poems of my newly adopted Holy Trinity: Emerson, Thoreau, and Whitman.

But now's not the time to get into all that, so back to Miss Harper's library. In addition to *Musings on Mother Earth*, the other notebook I found lying out on her desk that day was titled *The Miracle of Creativity*, and thumbing through it what I found were dozens of quirky little sayings similar to the ones I'd read while sitting along the bank of Willow Creek the week before. And just as I'd realized then, some were practical, such as, "*Always take the time to jot down an idea as soon as it comes to you, for if you don't then like a dream you can't quite remember it will quickly slip away."* And some were profound: *"Writing is an oxymoron of sorts, because you engage the process in a heightened state of awareness you are not at that moment even the least bit aware of."*

I mean, how damn lucky could a young writer get? There in my hands was an absolute treasure trove of intimate advice about, not only writing, but the very essence of creativity itself, and I'd been assigned the responsibility of organizing it into a cohesive whole. The very prospect was so incredibly exciting to me that I could hardly even contain myself.

And yet it was the notebook I had to search to find that would truly command my attention over the next few magical months, the one containing the rough draft of Miss Harper's new novel. I discovered it buried under a stack of old letters on the floor beneath her desk. It was smaller than the other two I'd found and bound in burnished leather, with the initials *E H* stamped into the lower right-hand corner, a notebook so old and worn that I couldn't help but wonder if maybe she'd written in it from the time that she was a child. Carefully opening the cover, I eagerly gazed down upon the hand-copied title, *Clouding Over*, the letters printed in a style as neat and tidy as everything else I'd seen in Ellen Harper's world.

And given that fact, you can well imagine the unbelievable shock I felt when I flipped to page one and found that the writing was such a chaotic mess that I could barely even *read* it! Honestly, she'd worked in a longhand script, and not only were many of the words so hurriedly scribbled that I couldn't even make out what they said, but others were completely scratched out, as were any number of entire sentences, and there were all these little arrows and stars connecting what seemed to me like random bits of passages and paragraphs. Even worse, as I then in a growing panic began to leaf through the rest of the notebook, I saw much to my horror that the *entire draft* had been composed in that same tumultuous fashion.

And it was then that I got my first real indication of just how demanding a job I'd taken on, and how incredibly difficult it was going to be for a novice like me to do justice to Ellen Harper's anxiously awaited new novel. I mean, finish by the time I started *graduate* school? Hell, not only would that be impossible, but given the virtually incomprehensible nature of the few pages I'd just scanned, I figured I'd be fortunate to finish at *all!*

✵ ✵ ✵

Later that afternoon I was sitting on the saggy old threadbare couch in my living room, having just done something I didn't do very often, but thoroughly enjoyed whenever I did. I'd just gotten stoned. And as I'm sure will come as no surprise, being high really intensified the state of anticipation I was hovering in, for I was just about to listen to an advance copy of an album that wasn't due to be released until three days later, on June 1st, an album that would not only become an instant cultural sensation, but would revolutionize rock'n'roll . . . the Beatle's *Sgt. Pepper's Lonely Hearts Club Band*. Ritchie Starkey had given it to me when I stopped by his record store on my way back from Ellen Harper's, and having spent the last half hour engrossed in trying to identify all the people on the cover, I was now ready to slip the disc onto the turntable, crank up the volume, and lose myself in the music.

And take me at my word, lose myself I did. As the opening chords of the title song came roaring through the speakers, I laid my head back, closed my eyes, and drifted off into a reverie inspired by the many brightly colored images that began to stream swiftly through my mind, one after another, and another, each more exotic and hypnotic than the last, and as potent with meaning as those in a dream.

But it was one image in particular that truly captured my imagination: "Look for the girl with the sun in her eyes and she's gone." For it reminded me all too vividly of how radiant Ellen Harper had been in the pictures I'd seen that morning. And the more that I thought back over each of those pictures in turn, the more that I realized there was something about Miss Harper I couldn't quite put a finger on, something . . . I don't know, vaguely familiar maybe, as if the idealistic young woman I'd gotten to know so well in *The Sky's the Limit* had suddenly come alive right before my very eyes. Or something like that. I wasn't really sure. In fact the only thing I knew for certain was that the feeling was so deep-seated and powerful that the music I was listening to gradually faded off into the background, and for what seemed like an oddly surreal passing of time all I was aware of was a surge of raw emotion as primal and yet puzzling as the very question of life itself.

Chapter Six

Tossing back the sheets and hopping to my feet, I headed out into the hallway and down to my trailer's one tiny spare bedroom, which I'd converted into a study. I'd brought Miss Harper's *Musings on Mother Earth* home to work on, and wanted to show Nicki a couple of the entries.

"Here we go," I said as I returned, plopping down onto the edge of the bed and opening the notebook in my lap. Nicki had her pillows all piled up behind her, and was propped up against them in her cute little cotton nightie, her light green eyes full of a tentative curiosity. She may not have understood my passion for this project. Nor was she particularly happy that I'd chosen to pursue it. But—and this is the part of the beauty of the woman—she was acutely aware of how important it was to me, and was therefore doing her best to be supportive.

"It's all carefully handwritten in chronological order," I explained, "starting from the time that she first left New York and became a really private person. For each entry there's a date, followed by a note on where she is and what she's doing, and then a reflection on nature. And I'm telling you, Nick, her feelings about the earth are so close to my own that it could've been me who wrote these words. I mean here, look at this one." And what I showed her was . . .

August 1946, high up along the front range of the Colorado Rockies, looking east out over the Plains.

*Insted of trying to conquer the earth,
we should be learning how to live in
harmony with her.*

After all, we are ultimately one and the same.

"So what do you think of that?" I wondered.

And she crinkled her nose, saying only that she wasn't quite sure what it meant.

"It means that we need to be more careful about how we treat the earth, because everything we do to her we're doing to ourselves as well. And that's exactly how it is too. On a deep biological level, we *are* the foods that we eat, and the air that we breathe, and the water that we drink. And since the earth provides us with all of those resources, and a *hell* of a lot more for that matter, we need to start showing her a little respect."

"Oh," she said. "I guess that makes sense, doesn't it? But are you sure that's what Miss Harper was trying to say?"

"Absolutely. She couldn't have been trying to say anything else."

"Or at least that's your opinion," she said a bit indignantly.

And so to eliminate the tension I could feel beginning to build, I flipped through the pages until I came up with an entry that to my way of thinking was so simple and direct that it couldn't have possibly meant anything other than precisely what it said. "Then how about this one?"

*May 1952, a thought that occurred as I
was working in the gaden just after a warm
spring rain.*

Living close to the earth is the most simple and effective way to establish a connection to the life force, that infinite impulse to be.

Her face screwed into a look of impatience. "That's a little too deep for me," she said. "Besides, I'm not as into all this nature stuff as you are. If you want to work on Miss Harper's notebook, then that's fine with me. But there's really no need for you to share all the details."

I kinda knew we'd been coming to this, but hadn't wanted to admit it. "And yet you are okay with me taking this job, right?"

"If that's what you feel that you have to do," she told me, folding her arms across her chest in a way that I took to be somewhat defiant.

And since I wasn't at all sure about how to respond to that, I decided to play it safe and talk around the issue. "So how'd your dad take it?"

"He was disappointed, of course, but mostly for my sake, not yours, because he knows that I worry about you wanting to be a writer. It simply too often leads to an unstable life."

"I can understand that," I told her, reaching out to caress her cheek—which she grudgingly allowed. "In fact when I called Robert Lawson to turn down that internship he touched on the very same subject, saying that I was passing up a great opportunity for the sake of what he considered to be a foolhardy risk. Other than that he was pretty nice about it, though."

She let out a lengthy sigh and slipped down under the covers, the gentle glow of the bedside lamp bringing out the red highlights in her auburn hair. "Let's not talk about it any more, okay? You've made your decision, and I can live with that. It's just going to take some time."

"You know what would help," I told her, setting the notebook down onto the floor and stretching out right alongside her, "is if you could stay over every now and again. I hate it that you have to go back to your dorm at night."

"Well, I hate it too," she said, staring up at the ceiling. "But that's just how it is. With the sorority house closed for the summer, and my parents dead set against me getting an apartment, my only choice was to go live there."

"I know that, but it all just seems so stupid. It's 1967, for God's sake. College girls shouldn't have curfews."

"But we *do*, Andy, so there's no sense complaining about it. If I'm not in by ten I'm going to be in *big* trouble, and I've worked too hard to succeed at this school to have a stain like that on my record."

I sure as hell couldn't argue with her there. She worked harder than anybody I'd ever known. So I simply let the matter drop, and after a bit of a cooling off period we snuggled in together . . . and before long we were making love. Nicki wasn't really into it, though. I could tell because her eyes remained sharply in focus the whole time. There was no abandonment, no release, no surrender to the moment. As embarrassing as it is for me to come right out and say it, she was simply going through the motions.

At dawn the next morning I took a spirited run, my pace fueled by the energy of conflicting emotions. I wanted so desperately to make Nicki happy, but the way things had been going over the past couple of days I couldn't help but wonder if that was even possible any more. I mean, she loved me. I had no doubt about that. But ever since I told her I'd decided to edit Miss Harper's new novel she'd seemed somehow . . . I don't know, removed, or distant in some way. It was almost as if she'd pulled deep inside to avoid facing the stark reality of the choice I'd made or something, and it bothered the hell out of me to see her like that—especially since I knew that it was my selfish need to follow my heart that was causing her such turmoil.

And yet just as I was about to completely surrender to that depressing train of thought, I heard a piercing screech and looked up to see a marsh hawk turning circles in the sky, its breast feathers brilliant in the light of the rising sun.

And suddenly aware of the warmth of that very same light upon my face, I drew in a deep breath of the cool spring air. And then another deep breath. And then another. And in a heartbeat I was simply striding along, step after carefree step, my thoughts as fluid as the water flowing ever forward at my side.

✧ ✧ ✧

"First of all I'd like to thank you for coming out this early," Ritchie Starkey said, taking a sip of coffee out of a silver thermos, his Rod Stewart-like hair freshly teased and sprayed. "Especially since we practiced so late last night."

"That's okay," Little John told him. "We've all pretty much known this was coming anyway, and as far as I'm concerned the sooner we talk about it the better. Right guys?"

And everybody else in the band simply nodded. We were sitting around an old wooden table at *The Hayloft*, the mid-morning sun shining dimly through the windows, each of us having received a call from Ritchie no more than an hour or so before.

"So you got in," Michael said, his voice strangely ambivalent.

"Yep," Ritchie told him with a shake of his head, as if he could still hardly even believe it himself. "I leave for basic training on the first of July, and that's really not as bad as you might think. I'm only gonna be gone for twenty-four weeks, and then a weekend every month, and I've already lined up a really good drummer who said he'd be willing to sit in for me."

"But what about your record store?" I wondered, knowing the pride that he took in managing it personally.

"I've got that covered too," he said. "So now it's just a matter of putting in my two years, and then getting on with my life. So I hope you're all willing to work with me on this, because I really don't want to drop out of the band."

"If only it was that simple," Little John interjected, reaching over to take Maureen by the hand, her chubby cheeks turning a bright red at his touch.

"What do you mean by that?" Michael asked him. He was a little hung-over, disheveled, and drinking an Alka-Seltzer, and I could tell by the way that his eyes suddenly narrowed that he was none too happy about any of this. Of course that was to be expected, given that unlike the rest of us he'd built his whole world around Willow Creek, and if the band was to break up he'd definitely suffer the most.

"What I mean is that Ritchie's not the only one worried about the draft," Little John explained, peering out at Michael from beneath his heavy brow. "I'm worried too, and Maureen's worried for me. So we've been tossing around some ideas, and right now I'm thinking about applying for a CO. What I'd like to do is work it off as a counselor at the VA hospital in Parkersburg, and that way I could commute and still stay in the band. But you know how that is. Hell, they might not even give me a CO, much less let me work it off wherever I want to."

"Well *godammit*," Michael said, pushing himself to his feet. "What in the hell are we supposed to do without a rhythm section?"

And that really set things off. "Now look here," Ritchie told him. "You have no damn right to get pissed off. You've got a bad knee, remember? Uncle Sam's not gonna come looking for you. And yet the rest of us are scramblin' for our fuckin' lives. So why don't you just calm down and let's deal with the situation as it *is*, and not as we *wish* it would be. All right?"

Michael ran his fingers through his tousled hair and paced back and forth for a minute or two, but eventually relaxed and sat back down. At which point Little John turned his thickly bearded face my way, drew in a pensive breath, and said, "Well, I guess that leaves you. What are you planning to do?"

"About what?"

"About the draft."

"You know," I admitted, looking at each and every one of my bandmates in turn. "I'm not really sure. I've been considering all sorts of options, but none of them seem to feel quite right. If I do get drafted, and I probably will, I could maybe attempt to lose enough weight to get under the limit, or try to prove that I suffer from depression or something. But I'm sure as hell not gonna run off to Canada, or do something really stupid like shoot myself in the foot or—what did that record salesman you know do, Ritchie?"

"He carried bars of soap around in his armpits for a couple of months," Ritchie said, "and it gave him some sort of a skin rot that got him out."

"Yeah, I'm not gonna do anything stupid like that. But the truth of the matter is, I don't really know what I'm gonna do yet."

I meant that too. I really did. There'd been so much else going on in my life that I simply hadn't given all that much thought to what I'd do if I was drafted. But even if I had. In fact even if I'd thought about it every day for the past year or two, not in my wildest dreams could I ever have imagined that things would turn out as they ultimately did.

Perhaps the most pivotal moment of the entire summer took place that very same afternoon. Of course I wasn't aware of that at the time, but in hindsight it seems kind of obvious.

I'd gone straight from the band meeting out to Ellen Harper's farmhouse, where I'd been sitting at her desk in the library finishing up my work on *Musings on Mother Earth*. And it wasn't just what Miss Harper had to say about nature that I was curious to find out about either. I also wanted to see what the notebook entries could tell me about her writing style. I'd already made a number of tentative attempts to begin reading the rough draft of her new novel, but hadn't even gotten through a whole page yet, so I was hoping that if I could develop a feel for the way that she expressed herself in a work that was essentially complete, I could then begin to see patterns in the maddening jumble of language I'd signed on to edit. Of course my best bet would have been to read through the rough draft of her *first* novel, *The Sky's the Limit*, so that I could then compare it to the published version I knew so well, but try as I may I simply couldn't find it. I'd made a thorough search of her desk, and her bookshelves, and even her filing cabinets . . . but hadn't had any luck whatsoever.

And yet it *had* to be there somewhere. I just knew it. And so did Jonathan Frazier. I'd gotten so frustrated about it not turning up that I'd called him for advice, and what he'd said was to keep looking because Miss Harper had never thrown *anything* away, not notes, or drafts, or even writing projects she'd given up on. Whatever she wrote she kept. No exceptions.

Anyway, I was sitting at her desk with *Musings on Mother Earth* spread open before me, the view out the bay window so incredibly enticing that I was having a hard time concentrating on the matter at hand. Or at least that's what I told myself way back then. At the moment, however, I've got to admit that it might have had at least a little something to do with the fact that I didn't want my work on that notebook to come to an end. It was so clearly written and well-organized that there wasn't any real editing for me to do, and as I got down to the last few entries I realized that I could have gone on reading them forever. So I was having a hard time letting go.

And therefore I made myself a bargain. I'd finish reading the notebook, copy out two of my favorite entries to keep in my wallet, and then move on to *The Miracle of Creativity*. And not only is that exactly what I did, but here are the two entries I've continued to carry with me up to this very day . . .

June 1960, hiking along the Ohio River on a lovely summer afternoon, the sky black from the smoke of a nearby refinery.

Fossil fuels are deposits of carbon impurities the earth has drawn out of the atmosphere.

It's her way of cleansing the air that we breathe.

And that gets me to thinking:

Why are we in our madness reversing that process?

And . . .

August 1962, on vacation in the Outer Banks of North Carolina, having just toweled off from a swim.

There's no better way to feel at one with the earth than to spend a day immersed in the sea.

Closing the notebook with a bit of a sigh, I then set it aside and began to stand up to stretch my legs . . . when out of nowhere I noticed something I hadn't seen before. There were binoculars tucked into an opening on the nearest bookshelf (right alongside the Audubon Society's *Birds of North America*), and taking them down I stepped up to the bay window and gazed through the lenses out into the valley below. And I've gotta tell you, it was breathtaking scenery too, the meadow grasses waving gently back and forth in the breeze, and hundreds of colorful wildflowers scattered about everywhere.

So thoroughly entranced did I become, in fact, that at first the movement along the creek made no impression on me whatsoever. It just seemed like a part of the natural landscape, like the ripples on the surface of the flowing water, and didn't really catch my attention at all . . .

Until suddenly there she was, as mystifying as an apparition, or a vision in a dream, a young woman strolling casually along the bank, stopping only to bend over now and again to pick a flower. She was wearing jean shorts and a plaid shirt knotted at the waist, and even though she was too far away for me to clearly make out her features, I could see that she had straw-colored hair and fair skin deeply reddened by the sun. And not only did it appear that she must have been gathering flowers for quite a while by then—the bouquet in her hand having grown almost too big for her to hold—but she seemed somehow . . . I'm not sure, oddly suited to the environment or something. You know, really comfortable, at ease—happy just being in the moment. And considering all the conflict I was embroiled in at the time, I kinda had to envy her that. Watching until she passed out of sight among the trees, I then stood there with the binoculars pressed to my eyes for at least another minute or two, hoping against hope that she'd come back into view. And why was I so anxious for her to return? Well if you've gotten to know me at all by now, the answer shouldn't come as any real big surprise: Because no sooner had I seen that young woman walking along the creek than I was overcome by a nearly mystical sense of fate, and it instantly became clear to me that I was somehow destined to get to know her, and really well too. Every fiber of my being testified to that. And oddly enough, even though she never did happen to reappear that day, the longer I stood there the more convinced I became that not only was she about to enter my life, but she was about to change it forever!

Hopeless romantic that I was back then, and continue to be to this day.

Chapter Seven

Leaning in over the bathroom sink, I eyeballed my bangs in the mirror, raised my scissors, and lopped off a good solid inch. I'd been cutting my own hair ever since I was a college freshman and first saw the Beatles on the *Ed Sullivan Show*. I mean they no sooner burst into "All My Loving" than a whole new world suddenly opened up to me, and I instantly knew that I simply *had* to be a part of it. So when I went home to visit my parents the following weekend I dropped by the local barbershop to see what the guy who'd been cutting my hair my whole life could do to turn me into a mop top. He was a crusty old fellow who'd been in business for more than forty years by then, with a striped pole out front and a hot towel for every man who came in for a straight-razor shave. And even though he specialized in flattops and crew cuts—and sported a super-short buzz cut himself—I figured he'd be up-to-date enough on the more current styles to help me achieve the effect I was after.

Wrong! No sooner had I told him what I wanted than he removed the clippings sheet from around my neck, tipped the barber chair forward, and summarily ushered me out of his shop, all the while mumbling under his breath about incorrigible youth and the total ruination of American culture. So what was I to do? I went back to my parent's house, wet my hair, and combing it straight down over my forehead I then started hacking away. And much to my surprise I was so pleased with the results that I haven't been back to a barbershop since.

Chuckling as I evened out the cut I'd just made, I then flashed back to how my parents had reacted when I first bopped into the living room looking like a member of the British Invasion. Dad merely lowered his newspaper and regarded me calmly, seemingly more bemused than anything else—while Mom's response was a bit more dramatic. Setting aside the *TV Guide* she'd been reading, she stood up out of her upholstered armchair and walked a circle around me to get a good look.

"You know," she said then, reaching up to smooth my cowlick, her eyes full of the kind of motherly affection that makes teenage boys highly uncomfortable. "The girls are really gonna love this, Andy. It makes you look like a scruffy little puppy."

And as that memory then slowly faded I couldn't help but gaze at my reflection and think about how lucky I was to have had Bob and Betty Adamson take me into their lives. I really mean that too. I simply couldn't have asked for better parents. Dad was a rather quiet, unassuming man, very even-tempered and somewhat bookish, a small town history teacher who liked nothing better than to spend the day at home reading. While mom, on the other hand, was a little more outgoing, more engaging if you will. She managed the office of the only family doctor in the entire county, and I doubt there was anyone within a thirty mile radius that she didn't know on a first-name basis.

And yet I didn't feel lucky just because my adoptive parents happened to be such down-to-earth people. It also had a lot to do with the fact that they loved each other unconditionally, and extended that same love to me. Not that there weren't still a lot of questions that I would've liked to have had answered. Because there were. So many, in all honesty, that in spite of the "genial sort of desperado philosophy" I'd embraced a couple of years before, not knowing who I really was, or where I really came from, occasionally continued to be a burden to me. And yet as I've already noted, it also made me feel somewhat unique. And beyond that it added a certain sense of intrigue to my self-image, an aura of mystery you might say—because the possibilities it led to were endless. I mean think about it. With no concrete past to define me, I could be pretty much anyone I imagined myself to be. And since I'm a natural-born dreamer anyway, over the years I'd conjured up any number of exciting scenarios.

So I guess you might say that as I finished trimming my hair on that spring morning in 67, I felt a certain ambivalence about being adopted. The practical part of me was still aching to know the story of my past, and yet the creative part of me was happy enough just being a blank page.

The young man . . . the young writer. Yang and yin. About as delicate a balance as there ever has been.

☆ ☆ ☆

"No wonder you named the band Willow Creek," Maureen said absently, raising a pudgy hand to push a few red curls off her cheek as she gazed out at a duck drifting by. "It's a beautiful little stream."

"Especially this section here," I told her, "because it's so secluded."

We were out on a walk a half mile or so down from my trailer, having stopped to sit along the bank while Little John went back to get some sandwiches he'd forgotten. And strangely enough it was a rather awkward moment for me, because Maureen had been uncommonly quiet all morning—her normally bright eyes dimly pulsing at best—and so I could tell that something was bothering her. It's just that I couldn't decide whether or not I should say anything.

And yet she was, after all, a really good friend, and about as open as anyone I'd ever known, so I eventually worked up my nerve and touched her on the shoulder to get her to look my way. "Are you okay?" I said then. "You seem a little subdued."

At first she didn't even react. She just sat there staring at me, her round and ruddy face as blank as could be . . . and then her eyes suddenly welled up and she burst into tears, falling into my arms and sobbing away. So I did what I'd like to think any good friend would do at a moment like that. I rocked her gently back and forth until she'd cried herself out, and then I pulled away just far enough to ask her if she felt like talking about it.

"Oh Andy," she said then, straightening up and drawing a tissue out of a pocket in the Mama Cass-like mumu she wore. "I'm just so scared. That's all." She paused for a few seconds to dab at her tears. "And even worse, I don't know how I'm *ever* gonna tell Little John."

"Tell him what?" I wondered, half-assuming that she must be pregnant.

Although as it turned out that wasn't the case at all. It had nothing to do with the promise of new life. Releasing a long and seemingly cathartic sigh, Maureen slowly gathered herself and said, "I was taking a shower yesterday morning and felt a lump in my breast, so I went to the University Health Center and all they could do was advise me to make an appointment with my doctor back home. And the sooner the better too, they said."

"And have you?" I asked quietly.

She gave me a slow nod and turned back to Willow Creek, her voice so soft as to nearly be a whisper. "I go in tomorrow," she said.

"Well chances are that it's just a cyst or something," I told her, doing my best to sound upbeat.

And she eased into a half-hearted smile. "Yeah, I know. I've done my research. And yet it's hard not to worry anyway. Two of my aunts died of breast cancer, and they were both pretty young when they got it. Not quite as young as I am, though. But still . . ."

And letting her voice trail off into the sound of the rushing water, she picked up a stone and gave it a mighty heave. Then she cast a wistful look my way, and leaned over to lay a hand on my knee. "So will you help me to come up with some way to tell Little John? You know how sensitive he is, and how he takes everything so seriously. He's really gonna have trouble with this."

She couldn't have been more right about that, because Little John was such a deep and philosophical fellow that I knew learning about a lump in Maureen's breast would take him way beyond his fears about her health and straight into the dark abyss of a serious existential dilemma. I'm not kidding either. Not even a little. It would most definitely cause him to question the very meaning of life itself, and why it is that we humans have to suffer so, and why it is that we have to die. That's just the kind of guy he was.

So I reached down to cover Maureen's hand with my own, and then I looked straight into her hopeful green eyes and said, "Not to worry. I'd be happy to help. And believe me, everything's gonna work out just fine. Don't ask me how I know that, but I do."

And the funny thing is, I was serious about that too. I really was. Somewhere deep inside I just knew that she'd be okay. And how could I be so sure about that? Because she had one hell of a strong spirit and a constantly positive attitude, and to my way of thinking that's about all any of us ever really need in order to stand up and face the many challenges life throws in our way. That and a little good luck. And even better yet, a whole lotta love.

☆ ☆ ☆

"I can't believe I lost track of the time," Nicki said, ducking out of my trailer and into a stormy night with my jean jacket held over her head. "There's no way we're going to make it."

"Sure we will," I told her. "As long as we don't hit every red light on the way."

Squishing across the yard to where Betsy was parked, we climbed in and I fired up the engine, which sputtered as usual and then, thankfully, caught. I was still a little worried about the windshield wipers, though, because the one on Nicki's side didn't work at all, and the one on mine was so erratic that I never knew exactly when it might come sweeping across in front of me. And yet all things considered it wasn't raining that hard, so I figured that as long as I drove carefully, we'd be okay. Flipping on the lights, I threw the gearshift into first and off we went.

"What's this?" Nicki said then. And I no sooner looked over to see her picking a birthday card up off the floor than my heart sank down into the pit of my stomach. I'd found it in my guitar case after a concert a couple of weeks before, and rather than being sensible and throwing it away I'd stuck it in my jean jacket and forgotten about it. The damn thing must've fallen out, and at a hell of a bad time too. Nicki was already upset as it was.

"Oh, it's just a card I got," I said casually. "No big deal."

"Who's it from?" she asked.

And seeing that she was about to open it, I decided I'd better take a more aggressive approach. "You don't want to do that," I told her.

"Why not?"

"Because it's from Julie."

And the silence that followed was so deep and ominous that a shiver ran up my spine. A seemingly endless moment passed . . . and then another. And then much to my relief Nicki released a pent-up breath and calmly asked me why the fact that the card was from Julie should keep her from wanting to read it.

"Let's just say," I began, hesitating for a heartbeat so that I could find the right words, "that she's become a little obsessive."

And hoping to blunt the shock of that news, I then reached over and turned on the radio, a move that I instantly regretted . . . because the song that came on was Aaron Neville's "Tell It Like It Is," and I wasn't the least bit prepared to do that.

Not that Nicki really gave me any choice. "A *little* obsessive?" she said in a barely controlled voice. "And just what do you mean by that?"

And that's when I realized that I could no longer avoid telling her the truth (although I must admit that I did give it a try). "Are you *really* sure you want to know?"

"Absolutely," she said.

Gripping the steering wheel in both hands and staring out through the rain at the oncoming headlights, I then steeled my nerves and let it all come out. "I've been getting cards and letters from her for the entire time that you and I've been together," I confessed, "but they've been so harmless up to now that I've never said anything about them because I didn't want to worry you."

The radio began to fade out at that point—the reception in the hills of southern Ohio notoriously poor at the time—so I reached over again to turn it off. And then I said, "This one's different though, Nicki. She makes veiled threats about being so desperate that if I don't let her back into my life she's gonna do something really drastic like hurt herself."

"She's going to *what?*" Nicki blurted, incredulous.

"Hurt herself," I repeated. "She didn't say how."

Nicki's dorm became faintly visible in the distance then, a beautiful but imposing ivy-covered stone structure, the light over the front entrance a sure sign that the door hadn't yet been locked. I knew that we were still cutting it too damn close for comfort, though, so I turned my attention back to the road and stepped on the gas . . .

And that's when it happened. With a sputter, a couple of jerks, and a really loud bang, good ol' Betsy simply gave out on me. Exchanging a quick glance with Nicki (who needless to say was clearly distraught), I then eased over onto the side of the road and we threw our doors open and jumped straight out into a sudden downpour, breaking into a run as soon as our feet hit the ground. And as I then heard a hissing and briefly turned back to see a cloud of steam rising up from Betsy's rear engine compartment, Nicki lost control and started to vent.

"That *goddam* awful car," she spat out between labored breaths. "My parents were right. It's nothing but a stupid old piece of *junk!*"

And even though I knew from past experience that she'd eventually calm down and feel bad about that outburst, right then every word that came out of her mouth was an arrow straight into my soul—because I was all too painfully aware that it wasn't just Betsy she was bitching about. The anger in her voice sprang from a much deeper source: Her fear of spending her entire future in a struggle to make ends meet with a wannabe writer like me.

Bounding up a series of brick steps and across a flagstone patio, we made it to the door just as the RD was walking up to lock it. And then without another word, or even a look, much less a touch, Nicki swiftly slipped inside and disappeared.

✫ ✫ ✫

Two yearlings, a bald eagle, and a bushy-tailed fox. That's a hell of a lot of sightings for one morning, I thought—although far from what I was actually hoping to see. Not quite yet ready to get down to work, I'd spent the last twenty minutes or so at the bay window in Miss Harper's library, staring out through her binoculars at the valley below. And while I'd truly enjoyed seeing all that wildlife, what I really had my heart set on was a glimpse of the young woman I'd seen picking flowers along the creek a few days before. In fact I'd spent a part of each of my two visits to Miss Harper's since then staring out into the valley in the hope that she'd reappear—only to be sorely disappointed both times.

Although I didn't get much of a chance to dwell on that, because the phone on Miss Harper's desk suddenly began to ring. Returning the binoculars to their slot on the bookshelf, I picked up the receiver and said hello.

"Good morning there, Andy," Jonathan Frazier replied. "I just thought I'd check in to see how the editing's coming. I'm a little more tied-up here than I'd anticipated, and probably won't get back to Ohio for at least another week, so I just wanted to make sure that you were getting along all right."

"I'm making real good progress thanks, Mr. Frazier," I told him. "I've already finished editing Miss Harper's book on nature, and I'm getting close to finishing up her book on creativity. And then once I'm done with that I'll get right to work on her new novel."

"Any luck finding the rough draft of *The Sky's the Limit?*"

"No, sir. No luck at all."

"Well don't lose heart. I meant it when I said that she kept everything she wrote. She was terribly proud of each and every last word. So that manuscript's got to be around somewhere, and therefore there's no need for concern. It's bound to turn up sooner or later. I'm certain of that."

"I sure hope you're right, Mr. Frazier," I said, unable to bring myself to tell him that if for some reason it *didn't*, then I'd have a god awful time trying to complete the job I was hired to do. I mean, he'd been so good to me that I simply didn't want to let him down. At least not yet anyway.

So rather than saying anything else about that missing draft, I switched to what was for me at that moment a much more compelling subject. "Oh and Mr. Frazier, while I'm thinking about it I'd like to ask you something. I couldn't help but notice the valley down below Miss Harper's house, and I was wondering if maybe she owned that land, because I've been thinking about taking a hike down there sometime, and wouldn't want to trespass on somebody else's property."

"You go right on ahead, Andy," he told me graciously. "That is indeed Miss Harper's land. Technically speaking, anyway. As far as she was concerned, however, it still belonged to the Murphys, the family she bought it from. It's somewhat of a long story."

"I see," I said—although I didn't. "So nobody'll care if I go down there?"

"I can't imagine why they would. The family does still live on a small farm at the east end of the valley, so you might possibly come across one of them. But if you do, simply introduce yourself and explain what it is you're doing there. They're very nice people, and Miss Harper was quite close to them, so I'm sure they won't mind. In fact if you do happen to run into one of the Murphys you can pass on a message from me. Miss Harper was particularly close to Bonnie Jo, the youngest child, and I'd like to ask her if she'd be willing to come to the house and organize Miss Harper's personal belongings. Lord knows I'm not up to that task."

"I'd be glad to do that, Mr. Frazier."

"Thank you, young man. I appreciate that. But please don't worry if there's no one around. It's certainly not a pressing concern, and I can easily take care of it whenever I get back there. Now if you'd be so good as to reassure me that you're getting along all right, I have a meeting to attend and am late as it is."

"Believe me," I told him. "I'm getting along just fine." Which of course wasn't entirely true. But then again, it was too early to let him know that I was struggling.

"Very well then," he said brightly. "Keep up the good work, and I'll return just as soon as I can."

Hanging up the phone, I then grabbed the binoculars and went back to gazing out into the valley—although as I'd come to expect there was no one in sight. You know what, though? At that moment I no longer even really cared, because thanks to my conversation with Mr. Frazier I was now more convinced than ever that I was destined to get to know the young woman I'd seen walking along down there. Whether or not she was Bonnie Jo Murphy, or another Murphy, or even a Murphy at all, I didn't know. But I did know that she'd soon be coming back into my life. In fact as far as I was concerned it was a foregone conclusion, a virtual act of nature, as inevitable as the pulling of the moon on the tides, or the budding of the trees in the spring. All that I had to do was sit back and allow the future to unfold on its own. And given that I'd just turned twenty-two, and felt that I had pretty much all the time in the world, I was certainly willing to give that a try. Besides, I knew that I'd been procrastinating long enough as it was, and needed to be getting to work. So I set the binoculars aside and shifted my focus to Miss Harper's chronicle of her life as a writer, *The Miracle of Creativity*.

And what a wonderful book it was turning out to be too. Or maybe I should say what a wonderful compilation, since as I mentioned earlier it was simply a collection of quirky little sayings like the ones I'd first read while sitting alongside Willow Creek. The only problem was, it was a *random* collection, and that meant that it needed a hell of a lot of editing.

That was perfectly all right with me, though, because I now fully believed that I was up to the challenge. In fact each of the entries I'd come across so far had easily fallen into one of the two categories I'd identified from the start. They'd been either: 1) Practical, or 2) Profound. And that's exactly how I'd decided to set up the book.

I've got to say that I was having a lot of fun with it too, in great part due to the fact that I was learning so much about being a writer. I mean, people paid thousands of dollars to take classes from famous authors, and here I had free access to the handwritten notes of one of the most famous of all. And as I immersed myself in those notes on that early June morning, these are the two I came across that made the biggest impression on me . . .

Be sure to keep a notebook and pen by your bed, for the dreamlike state between consciousness and sleep is extremely fertile ground indeed.

And . . .

No matter what form an author's work might take, its true essence, or in other words its absolute energy, comes from beyond the realm of this world. And therefore on the deepest and most intimate level, writing is a metaphysical (I might even dare say "spiritual") endeavor.

And I've gotta tell you, as soon as I read that second entry I sat straight up in my chair, because not only did it speak directly to my heart, but it also reminded me of how closely connected Miss Harper and I both were to the Transcendentalists, who'd so devoutly believed in "eidolon," the spiritual energy behind all physical reality. It's what Emerson was referring to when he wrote that true poetry "is an expression of the Divine," and Whitman when he described it as "a reflection of the soul."

And given that I'd spent the past few days in a heightened state of inspiration thanks to such eye-opening concepts, and better yet I had at least another couple of days worth of equally stimulating material to look forward to, I was momentarily able to rise above my fears about editing Miss Harper's new novel, and was actually feeling pretty damn good about the way my work was going.

Now if only I could get Nicki to feel good about it too.

Chapter Eight

Reaching out to adjust the side mirror of the band's equipment van—our iconic old Wonder Bread truck—Little John then picked up the Jungle Larry safari hat he always wore when he drove it and smashed it down onto his massive head of dark hair. We'd just finished loading the amp we'd taken in to be repaired, and were now heading back to *The Hayloft* to set up for our concert that night. And I'm happy to say that in spite of all the trauma surrounding the lump in Maureen's breast, Little John was holding up pretty damn well. My advice to her had been to include him in the process from the very beginning, because that way he wouldn't have the chance to just sit around and stew about it. And that's exactly what she'd done. She'd taken him with her when she'd gone in to see her hometown doctor, and then when she'd returned the next day for tests. And she was now including him in the research she continued to do as they waited to hear the results. Not that he hadn't lapsed into a bit of a funk, mind you. It's just that it wasn't nearly as deep as I'd feared, and all things considered it appeared to be more philosophical than fatalistic.

Case in point: "So why do you think it is that some people get sick and others don't?" he said, his deepest eyes fixed firmly on the road.

"Hard to say," I replied. "In fact I'm not even sure we're capable of knowing something like that."

"But you do think there's a reason?" he wondered. "Or is it just serendipity? You know, the luck of the draw."

"I don't know, Little John. I really don't. I mean if somebody smokes their whole life and then gets lung cancer, that's certainly no surprise. But when

somebody who leads a healthy lifestyle gets sick, especially somebody really young…
well again, I just don't know."

We were coming to a red light, so he geared down and braked gently to
make sure that the amp didn't shift. "And yet sometimes it just doesn't seem
fair," he said, turning to give me a wan smile. "Does it?"

And all I could do was say no, it doesn't. "But look at it this way. When it
comes to Maureen there's still a damn good chance that she isn't even really sick
after all, so it's probably best not to worry too much."

The light turned green at that point, so he shifted into first and eased down
onto the accelerator. "Easy for you to say," he then muttered, his eyes once again
on the road. "But not so easy for me."

✵ ✵ ✵

It was one of those letters I couldn't even wait to get inside to open. So there
I stood, right next to the beat-up old mailbox on the shoulder of the rural road
I lived on, having just read a return address that said . . .

Local Board No. 14
Federal Building
1200 Liberty Avenue
Columbus, Ohio 43221

And as a flatbed hauling timber then rumbled on by, the wind in its wake
whipping the clothes around my body, I tore off one end of the envelope and
slipped out the official-looking notice inside, my head reeling from the fateful
words at the top of the page.

Greetings:

You are hereby directed to present yourself for an Armed Forces
Physical Examination . . .

And you know what? Even though I'm not a person who often uses vulgar language, at that moment it seemed entirely appropriate. "Oh fuck," I said to myself. "I'm screwed."

✶ ✶ ✶

The funny thing about performing is that there are times when you're in such a groove that you're more or less on automatic pilot, and therefore not nearly as conscious of the music flowing out of you as you are of the impact that it's having on your audience. And that's exactly what I experienced that Saturday night. We were singing a sentimental love song I'd written, "May I Have this Dance?" It's about a widowed professor who's getting up there in years and doesn't want to spend the rest of his life alone. And even though I was only twenty when I wrote the song, and the average age of my audience couldn't have been a hell of a lot more than that, it appeared to be having the desired effect. The few people slow-dancing had melted into each other's arms, and the ones watching the band were swaying gently back and forth to the beat, the men looking somewhat somber and the women all dewey-eyed.

And then of course there was Julie. She was off to my right, her long and lithe body pressed up against the front of the stage, and so deeply moved by the song that she was crying. Or at least that's what I hoped she was crying about. Either way, there was no sign of the desperation she'd confessed to in the birthday card she'd slipped into my guitar case. She simply looked as if she was overcome by emotion. And again, I was really hoping it was the song.

Most of my focus, however, was drawn to a back corner of the room, where there was a young couple standing in the shadows, so deep in conversation that they paid no attention to the band whatsoever. And even though they remained a respectful distance apart, and neither showed any outward sign of affection for the other, I was still none too happy about seeing them together. Nicki sure did look lovely, though, her long auburn hair flowing down across her shoulders and her eyes so full of life that they damn near sparkled.

And that's kind of what worried me, because she'd been spending an awful lot of time with the guy she was talking to, and in my opinion they got along entirely too well. His name was Joseph P. Wentworth III, and at the risk of sounding paranoid he was every bit the man I'd recently been fearing Nicki wished I could be. A pre-Law major with his eye set on politics. President of his fraternity. Undergraduate representative on the Faculty Senate. A real up-and-comer.

He and Nicki had met in the early spring, when they'd both been appointed to the Campus Greek Life Committee, and they'd hit it off from the very start, in great part due to their shared backgrounds and similar values. In fact she'd fairly gushed about him at dinner on the day they'd first been introduced (totally oblivious to my not-so-subtle attempts to get her to talk about something else). And ever since then their on-campus activities had constantly thrown them together.

So was I jealous? Was that it? I can't honestly say. I mean, Nicki had certainly never given me any reason to be. And yet there's no denying that seeing her huddled in the shadows with Mr. Big Man on Campus was making me really uneasy. So I turned to an old trick I often relied on when something was bothering me: I tried to think about something else. In this case the odd assortment of fans the band always attracted. And I'm talking seriously eclectic here. We not only pulled in the standard university blend of long-haired freaks and buttoned-downed Greeks, but also a faithful local contingent of blue-collar workers and farmers. All of whom at that moment, I'm proud to say, seemed totally lost in the music.

Except for Nicki and Joseph P. Wentworth of course. They continued to be locked into each other at the back of the room, and that continued to bother the hell out of me—although I could tell from the look on the faces in the crowd that I was doing a good job of masking my emotions in song.

And with that as inspiration I was finally able to get control of myself and refocus my attention, putting everything I had into a series of sweetly melodic chords, and a tender lyric about the ever ageless power of love.

For whatever that was worth.

✲ ✲ ✲

Riddled with second thoughts, I opened the door that led out of Miss Harper's living room and into the hallway behind it, hoping that I might find the rough draft of her first novel in one of the three rooms back there. The only problem was, I felt really guilty about snooping around, as if maybe I was betraying Miss Harper's trust, or even violating her somehow. And because of that I made a pact with myself. I'd look only on surfaces, and not in any closets or drawers. And if by some chance that draft failed to turn up, then whoever Jonathan Frazier finally hired to organize Miss Harper's personal possessions could continue the search from there.

The first room I entered was a spare bedroom with full bath, and just like what I'd seen of the rest of the house it was simply and rustically furnished. A king-sized bed with an old oak headboard. A matching bedside table. And a mission-style dresser with an antique mirror above it. I only ended up staying there for a minute or two, though. First of all because there wasn't anything even remotely resembling a manuscript in sight, and secondly because it was pretty obvious from the cufflinks on the dresser and the tie slung over a doorknob that it was essentially Mr. Frazier's room.

So I wandered on down the hall to the next room, which also turned out to be a spare bedroom, although this one had been converted into a music studio. And what a *seriously* cool place it was too! Along with a variety of really nice guitars, there were mandolins and fiddles and banjos galore. Not to mention the music stands, and capos, and other accessories scattered about. I even saw a four-track mixing console, and a few basic but functional mikes. I mean, I'd known from Miss Harper's record collection that she was really into music, but up to that point I'd had no idea just how deeply into it she'd been.

And yet in spite of how impressed I was by Miss Harper's music studio, it was in the master bedroom at the end of the hall that I made my greatest discovery. It wasn't exactly the one I was *hoping* for, mind you, although it was pretty damn exciting nonetheless. On a small wicker table next to a big brass bed lay a slender book with a plain white cover, and leafing through it what I found was a series of poems, each fluidly and elegantly handwritten. Skimming over them, I read about everything from the monastic solitude of the writing life to the joyous unburdening of middle age.

But it wasn't until I was almost to the end of the book that I came across a poem that touched me so deeply that I stopped to read it carefully. It had to do, not surprisingly, with the act of writing, and its whimsical title belied what I considered to be a work of amazing insight.

Who Would've Known?

*Writing is both a solemn ritual,
and a day at the funhouse,
a sentence to prison,
and a walk on the beach.
The muse with a thousand faces.*

*Surrender yourself to the life force within,
and a wave of inspiration will sweep you
away.*

Pretty nice, huh? I sure thought so. Unfortunately it had such a positive feel to it that the next poem I turned to, the final one in the volume, caught me completely off guard— mainly because it was so foreboding that it made me wonder if Miss Harper might have written it due to the simple fact that she'd somehow suspected that she didn't have much longer to live.

December

The weight of winter is upon me,
sky heavy with snow,
and boughs bent low,
smothered in ice.

My bones are a burden.

The earth tugs at my soul.

Closing the book and setting it back onto the wicker table, I slowly turned and walked out of Miss Harper's bedroom, gently pulling the door closed behind me. And as I then made my way back down the hall, across the living room, and up the stairs to her library, I found much to my surprise, and embarrassment, that there were tears streaming down my cheeks. And even though at the time I had no idea as to why, I certainly do now, and I'll forever be thankful that at least on an unconscious level I was finally beginning to piece things together.

✻ ✻ ✻

Blinking in the light that streamed in through the big bay window, I stepped up into Miss Harper's library and was heading on over to her desk . . . when suddenly I could've sworn that I heard somebody singing. So I stopped to listen, and sure enough I was right. There was a faint but unmistakable voice coming from somewhere down below the back of the house.

And as my heart then began to race, I immediately hustled on across the room and looked out . . . and lo and behold there she was, a young woman pulling weeds in the uppermost of the three terraced gardens. She was wearing work boots, canvas pants, and a faded denim shirt. And even though my every instinct told me that she was the same young woman I'd seen the week before, I of course couldn't be completely sure, because she'd been too far away at the time for me to get a good look at her face. Hell, for that matter I couldn't even see it at the moment, since there was a big old straw hat in the way. She certainly did have a beautiful voice, though. It was clear, and strong, and melodic. And in spite of the fact that I didn't recognize the tune, it was so catchy that I found myself wanting to hum along.

Although I never did get the chance, and I'll tell you why too—because in that instant I realized something that gave me pause. The young woman's straw hat looked an awful lot like the one that Miss Harper had on in my favorite picture of her. Remember? It sat next to a copper jar on the bookshelf and showed her in what must have been her early forties, smiling up at the camera as she worked among tomato vines.

And swinging around to take a look at that picture not only confirmed my theory, but it also gave me kind of an eerie feeling, because the young woman was working in what appeared to be the same section of the garden Miss Harper had been working in too. And that was entirely too coincidental not to have some sort of a deeper meaning. That is, if you believe in stuff like that. Which I did (and for that matter still do).

Regardless, I was so overcome by the feeling that I was destined to get to know that young woman that I desperately wanted to call out to her—and yet unfortunately I couldn't because the window didn't open. And that left me no choice but to hurry on back down the stairs, through the living room and kitchen, and out the back door . . .

Only to find that she was already gone. Scrambling along the path that led down through the forest to the gardens, I discovered a bucket of weeds at the end of the row she'd been working in, and yet she herself was nowhere to be seen.

But then, just as I as beginning to wonder if maybe my imagination had finally gotten the better of me, I heard a loud creaking and turned to see an old wooden shed hidden back among the trees, its well-weathered door swinging oh so slowly open . . . and out she came, a fresh-faced young country girl wiping the sweat off the back of her neck with a red bandana.

"Well hey there," she said with a twang and a smile. "I've kinda been wonderin' when we were gonna meet." And then, with a wink. "It simply *had* to happen, ya know."

Boy did I.

Chapter Nine

The following Thursday, June 15th, ended up being one of the benchmark days of the entire summer, because it was then that I finally made my first real breakthrough in reading the rough draft of Miss Harper's new novel. Frustrated about having made so little sense of the first few pages, I was absentmindedly thumbing through the rest of it when I suddenly came across a number of clearly written passages. And after that it took me less than an hour's work to realize that, as I'd fully expected, the story was no doubt the autobiographical sequel to *The Sky's the Limit*, which had ended with young Eleanor Taylor signing a publishing contract in New York, and then returning in triumph to the Appalachian foothills of her youth.

Unfortunately, what I stumbled upon that Thursday morning wasn't nearly as uplifting. From what I could tell it was now a year or so later, and Eleanor was back in the city to promote what was turning out to be a runaway best seller. The only thing is, she didn't want to be there, not in the least . . . because she'd already become seriously disillusioned with literary fame and fortune.

And wouldn't you know it, within seconds of figuring that out I got a call from Jonathan Frazier. He wanted to let me know that he was in the process of winding up his business affairs and would be flying back to Ohio the following Monday. And to me the timing, besides being ironic, couldn't have been more perfect—since I was now able to assure him in all honesty that I was actually making a little headway.

"It once again appears to be a fictional account of her own life," I told him.

"Indeed," he replied. "That much I've already assumed. For even though Miss Harper rarely discussed a work in progress, and I was therefore never made aware of the particulars of the story, I do know that she was comfortable only when writing about what she herself had personally experienced. Because, as she once explained, it was the only 'authentic' subject matter she had."

"Well if that's really what she was like, then I'd have to say that she didn't care much for being famous, did she?"

"My goodness no. She found it abhorrent. And it wasn't just that so many people she thought were her friends suddenly became envious and spiteful, or that others she hardly even knew began to fawn all over her purely in the hope of personal gain. It was first and foremost her loss of privacy altogether. She was, after all, a fairly quiet and introspective person, and being thrust so abruptly into the glare of the spotlight quite simply overwhelmed her. Besides, in her opinion the public's idealized perception of her was highly inaccurate to begin with, and therefore she felt that she could never, *ever* hope to live up to it."

"Is that why she became so reclusive?"

"In great part I must say that it was. At first she regarded avoiding celebrity as a rather new and exciting game, although it quite rapidly became a serious nuisance, in that no matter where she went, or what she did, both her fans and the press hounded her without mercy. And that's when she decided that perhaps she should just build a private country retreat and simply leave it all behind. It even got to the point that she was thankful for the many vicious rumors that then began to circulate around her. I'm sure you've heard them. The breakdown. The stroke. The disfigurement. Et cetera. People were so certain that a catastrophe must have befallen her that as the years passed she could move freely about without attracting attention. Whether she was traveling the world or merely going into town, as long as she dressed like a simple country girl and kept a low profile, nobody realized who she was."

"But wasn't she lonely?" I wondered.

"At times she was indeed lonely. But you must remember, at heart she was an extremely independent woman, and unbeknownst to the general public she had a number of very dear friends, among them the Murphys I mentioned last week. Which reminds me. I went ahead and called Bonnie Jo Murphy, and she's not only agreed to sort through Miss Harper's personal belongings, but also to continue to maintain the gardens, a labor of love that both she and Miss Harper greatly enjoyed sharing. As I believe I've told you, they'd grown quite close."

"Funny you should bring that up," I said, "because I was in the library the other day and happened to look out and see her pulling weeds. So I went on down and introduced myself as you suggested, and she told me that she'd already talked to you and had been expecting to meet me."

"Lovely young lady, isn't she?"

"*I'll* say!"

And I must have come across as a little too enthusiastic, because Jonathan Frazier then offered a word of caution. "Well you behave yourself, young man," he said in a fatherly tone. "You have a tremendous amount of work to accomplish, and I wouldn't want to see you distracted."

"Not to worry, Mr. Frazier," I promised. "I've had a steady girlfriend for more than two years now, and it's beginning to look like we'll be together for many more years to come."

And strangely enough, as much as I believed that when I spoke those words, they no sooner began to echo in my ears than for some reason I wasn't so sure. In fact my voice sounded downright hollow, as if maybe what I'd said didn't come from my heart at all, but from a part of me that had somehow been *programmed* to think that way. And that was *very* disturbing to me. Very disturbing indeed.

One of the real advantages of living so close to Willow Creek was that there were any number of ideal spots where I could sit and play the guitar, or read, or simply just hang out and think—which is exactly what I was doing later on that very same afternoon. The fact that I might not really love Nicki anymore was so troubling to me that I realized I'd better try to sort out my feelings, so I'd settled down in the shade of a pine bough to gaze out at the flowing water and do just that.

And yet as is so often the case, life had a few ideas of its own, and things didn't end up quite like I'd planned. We'd had so much rain over the past few months that the creek was running really high, and I was marveling at how incredibly fast the current was moving . . . when suddenly I noticed a little pool of still water trapped between a partially submerged log and the shoreline. Intrigued, I stood up and walked on over to check it out.

And no sooner had I bent down to give it a good look than I saw my own reflection staring right back up at me. Shaggy blond hair. Inquisitive eyes. And a decidedly puzzled expression. My initial reaction was to break into a grin, because in spite of the vast amount of time I'd spent down by Willow Creek, I couldn't recall ever having seen my image shimmering on its surface before.

And yet it wasn't long until I succumbed to my usual fate whenever I dwelt on my reflection. I began to consider the many questions surrounding the fact that I was adopted, and would therefore never have the chance to really get to know the person whose eyes were at that moment locked onto mine. No matter how deeply I delved, there would forever be a part of me that remained a total mystery.

Not that I wasn't thankful for the part of me that had been shaped by my upbringing, mind you. Because I was. In fact, sentimental fool that I am, I'd have to say that I felt absolutely blessed to have been raised in the small town world of Bob and Betty Adamson, and right then I missed them both so much that I would've liked nothing better than to drive on up to see them and give them a hug.

And yet much to my regret I couldn't do that, because they were living in Germany for the summer. Dad had been awarded a professional development grant to research the methods by which history was being taught in the Munich public schools, so mom had taken a leave of absence from her job in the doctor's office and off they'd gone, not to return until just before Dad's school year began in late August. And that meant that no matter what I had to deal with until then, whether identity problems, or girlfriend problems, or even just the problem of trying to decide what in the hell I should do about my future, I had no one to turn to for help except the person I was staring at in a pool of still water. And on the deepest and most intimate level, the guy remained an absolute stranger to me. So needless to say, as a maple leaf slowly drifted in and distorted my image, I was feeling pretty damn alone in this world.

Straightening up and returning to my seat beneath the pine bough, I then lay back on the grass and stared up into what on that afternoon seemed to me to be a depressingly infinite and empty sky, the rain-swollen rapids rushing ever on by, oblivious to the fact that I was even lying there at all.

✲ ✲ ✲

"Just one more minute," the preppy college girl behind the front desk said with a smile. Then she returned to the book she was reading.

So I looked back down at the magazine I'd been mindlessly flipping through, *Cosmopolitan*. It was either that or *Seventeen*, neither of which really appealed to me. That was okay, though, because I hadn't had a whole lot of time to kill anyway. Having come into town to buy the Bee Gee's first album—I was blown away by their three-part harmonies—I'd whimsically decided to stop by Nicki's dorm to say hi. There was a freshman orientation program going on at the university, and she'd been so busy preparing for the Campus Greek Life presentation that night that I'd hardly even seen her for the past few days. So I just wanted to wish her good luck. The problem was, during the week men were only allowed in the women's rooms from three to seven. Otherwise we had to stay in the lounge, where there was absolutely nothing to do except leaf through the few boring magazines scattered about.

"Okay," the desk clerk said then. "Three o'clock on the nose. I'll call up and tell her you're coming."

"No wait," I said, popping to my feet and stepping up in front of her. "I'd like it to be a surprise. I'm kind of a romantic that way."

"But sir," she said, her prim little mouth tightening ever so slightly, "our policy is—"

And as she then broke off I cringed to see what had become an occupational hazard for me: the light of recognition in her eyes. "You're that guy that sings for Willow Creek, aren't you?"

"Not at the moment," I told her. And I wasn't being rude either. I just didn't like being pinned to that image.

She certainly didn't appear to be offended, though. In fact she reacted to my comment with a giggle. "Well I just *love* your music," she gushed. And then, coyly. "So I guess maybe it'd be okay if I let you go on up. Don't forget that you have to leave the door open, though. And you will knock before going in, won't you?"

"Scout's honor," I said, flashing the appropriate sign.

And I was true to my word too. I did knock . . . just not right away. For as I came down the hall I saw that Nicki's door was already cracked open, and as I then got closer I could hear her talking to some other girl.

"So what do you think?" Nicki asked.

"Too conservative," the other girl told her. "I'd go for something a little more sexy if I were you."

"*Sexy?*" Nicki wondered. "*Really?*"

"I don't know why not. You do want to make an impression, don't you?"

"Well of *course* I do. But . . . *sexy*? Are you sure?"

"You only go around once in life, you know."

And I've got to admit, that entire conversation left me completely baffled. I mean, Nicki had been involved in any number of official presentations since we'd been dating, and I'd never once known her to second-guess the way she was dressed. Regardless, I thought it was about time for me to make my presence known, so I gave the door a quick rap.

"Just a second," Nicki called out. And then I heard a flurry of activity before . . . "Okay, you can come on in now."

And the look on her face as I then walked into that room will stay with me forever. I'm telling you she was absolutely *shocked!* In fact her eyes went so wide that I might have been an alien creature or something. And the other girl's eyes went even *wider!!* Although that didn't surprise me. Not in the slightest. Her name was Maryann McNulty, and of all the girls in Nicki's sorority she was by far the most outspoken in her belief that our relationship would never survive the devastating blow of me forming a folk-rock band. In fact there were times when I suspected that she might even have been *plotting* to break us up. And therefore it was no wonder that she'd reacted so dramatically, because she knew that I didn't care for her and wouldn't be all that happy to see her.

Which might help to explain why she immediately looked at her watch and excused herself, saying that she had to get on over to the Student Center to help set up for the night's events. And as she then scurried off, making sure to leave the door ajar, Nicki turned to me and said, "She can actually be a very nice person, Andy. You just have to give her a chance."

And you know, I don't often get pissy. Really, I don't. But Maryann McNulty had said so many nasty things about me that I was just about to lose control and really tear into her . . . when suddenly from out in the hall there came this seriously pumped up male voice. "*Hey* there! It's *show*time! Are . . . you . . . *READY*?!"

And who then appeared in the open doorway but none other than Joseph P. Wentworth III, his cheeks instantly turning about ten shades of red. And that's when it hit me . . . and hit me *hard*. Nicki hadn't been dressing for the incoming freshmen. Nicki had been dressing for *him*!

☆ ☆ ☆

Running down the backwoods Jeep road that paralleled Willow Creek, I set my pace to match that of a little pine cone that was bobbing along on the current. It was odd to be out running on a Friday night, but I felt that I simply had to get in a few miles. Nicki was at that very moment giving her presentation at freshman orientation, and even though she'd made it perfectly clear that I was welcome to come and listen, I was so upset about the incident in her dorm room that afternoon that I wanted to be alone. So you'd think that as I ran along I'd be worrying about her being with Joseph P. Wentworth III, or maybe even questioning the state of our relationship in general . . . but I wasn't. I was remembering the first time that I'd truly become aware of my own mortality.

It happened when I was fifteen and my mom took me in to see the doctor whose office she managed to get my yearly physical. I was sitting in the waiting room afterwards, kind of half-listening as she consulted with Dr. Miller back in the examination room, and even though I couldn't quite make out what they were saying, I thought I heard a note of concern in her voice. And as she then came through the door and I saw the look in her eyes, I knew for *sure* that something had to be wrong.

"Now I don't want you to worry," she said, taking the chair next to me and giving me a hug. "But Dr. Miller picked up what he thinks might be a heart murmur, and he'd like to keep an eye on you for the next six months or so."

And I was certainly in no position to argue with that. So every few weeks I had to go in to the doctor's office, strip to the waist, and get hooked up to an EKG machine that printed out a record of my heartbeat, the very rhythm of my being. And even though I'd expected that to be the ultimate pain in the ass, it wasn't. In fact I *loved* it! And how could that possibly be? I'll tell you . . . because of every post-pubescent boy's ultimate fantasy, the beautiful and sexy Nurse Nancy. She was Dr. Miller's assistant, and the one who actually administered the EKG. And I can't even begin to tell you how heavenly that was, lying there on the examination table as Nurse Nancy hovered over me, a sweetly fragrant angel in white, her cool hands fluttering softly all around my bare chest as she rubbed on soothing dabs of conducting gel and attached little round suction-cup sensors. I mean, talk about a host of sensations that I'd never *known* before! Each and every little touch sent waves of pleasure coursing throughout my body, and the overall effect was so incredibly erotic that in spite of how embarrassing it was I couldn't keep from responding, if you know what I mean. And the fact that Nurse Nancy gave subtle signs of noticing only made the entire experience just that much more exciting!

Although just as Dr. Miller had suspected, the end results were a bit of a downer. I did indeed have a heart murmur. It wasn't terribly serious, though, just a single valve that didn't quite close all the way, causing a faint *whoosh* in the rhythm of my heart. And there wasn't anything anybody could do about it anyway, except to check it every now and again to make sure that it didn't get worse. Which of course was perfectly all right with me. In fact there are no words to express how much I looked forward to my periodic EKG's. They were an absolute *highlight* in my adolescent life. As you can well imagine.

But you know, those few wonderful moments with Nurse Nancy weren't the only good thing to come out of discovering that I had an irregular heartbeat. It's also what caused me to take up running. Seriously. My dad sat me down on the night that I got back from my physical and the two of us had a bit of a man-to-man talk. What he told me was that we all face challenges as we go through this life, and the best way to deal with them is to be pro-active—or in other words meet them head-on. So that's exactly what I did. First I read every medical reference book I could get my hands on, and then based on what I learned from them I put myself on a heart-healthy diet and began to go for a daily run. And even though I'd never really been all that athletic before, I took to it like a newborn dolphin takes to the sea. In fact unlike so many other people who run on a regular basis, I've never once thought of it as a discipline. From the moment that I first laced up my Adidas and headed out my parent's front door, it's simply been a natural part of who I am, and what I do, like breathing, or making music, or writing.

And it was in the midst of the solitude of that very first run that I felt my heart thumping and realized that no matter what measures I took to strengthen it, the day would come when it would suddenly stop beating, and the earthly me would cease to be. And yet as strange as it may seem, that didn't bother me at all. Quite the contrary. It merely reinforced a belief I'd held so deep inside for so long that I assumed it had been with me since birth: My soul would live on forever. I just *knew* it! A person's physical life is ephemeral. It comes and goes. That's simply the way it is. But the spiritual energy that empowers that life exists throughout the whole of eternity.

And as I then felt a drop of rain on my face and eased back into that Friday evening in 67, I noticed that even though I hadn't been conscious of the world around me for at least the past half mile, I was still running right alongside that little pine cone in Willow Creek, the two of us continuing along on our separate adventures ever into the vast unknown.

I was really rollin' to the rhythm of a rockabilly tune when I was struck by the thought that the band had never sounded quite so good as it did that night. Not that we didn't sound good every night, mind you. Because we did. Maureen saw to that. In fact it never ceased to amaze me how much her Earth Mother spirit influenced the music we made. From the moment that she first stepped up behind the soundboard, everything we played took on a deeper, richer, and more abundant energy. There was even something vaguely magical, or even mystical about it, as if each and every last note had to somehow be drawn through her before it could make its way over into the speakers, and then on out into the world.

And yet in spite of all that Maureen added to our music every single time that we played, our sound that Saturday night was especially robust and vibrant. And there was a really good reason for that too. She'd gotten her test results back from the doctor, and the lump in her breast had turned out to be nothing more serious than a build-up of glandular tissue. No big deal whatsoever. She could now go on back to her daily life without the spectre of death shadowing her every move.

And oh how lovely she looked now that her worries were gone, bopping along to the beat as she worked her wonders at the back of the room, her green eyes shining brightly and her chubby cheeks so aglow that they were downright cherubic. And even though the band laid out any number of distinct rhythms for her to choose from, it was to the unbelievably light and bouncy bottom line of Little John's bass that she moved. That was as obvious to me as the brilliant aura of unbridled joy that surrounded them both.

Yes indeed, it was a fine night for making music. It was a fine night for being in love. And it was a fine night for embracing *all* the promise the future could possibly hold.

It's just that because I hadn't spoken with Nicki since I'd stormed out of her dorm room the day before, and for the first time ever she'd failed to show up at *The Hayloft* to hear us play . . . it wasn't a fine night for me.

✧ ✧ ✧

I'd never gone out to Miss Harper's on a Sunday morning before, but I really needed something to do to keep my thoughts busy. I'd called Nicki as soon as I got home from my gig, and even though it had to have been after one by then the phone had just kept on ringing. So needless to say I hadn't slept very well, two or three fitful hours at the most. And when I'd then called again that morning and she *still* didn't answer, my imagination had kicked into overdrive. So I was looking for something other than Nicki to focus on in order to settle it down.

And that's how I came to be standing on Miss Harper's screened-in porch, entering the elaborate security code into the keypad alongside the front door, so mentally and emotionally beat down that it seemed damn near surreal when the door swung open and I was greeted by the sound of music. Somebody was strumming an acoustic guitar. Following the sound through the living room and down the back hallway to Miss Harper's music studio, I then paused just outside the open doorway as the strumming was replaced by some spirited finger-picking. And that's when I was overcome by curiosity and decided to step into view . . . only to have my eardrums nearly split by a high-pitched scream as Bonnie Jo Murphy then glanced up and saw me.

"Good *god*," she said after she'd calmed down a bit. "Don't *ever* do that again, Andy. I almost jumped outta my skin."

"Sorry," I told her. "I don't know what I was thinking. Are you gonna be okay?"

"As soon as I catch my breath," she muttered, setting the guitar down onto the floor and leaning back to inhale deeply.

And in the following silence I couldn't help but notice two things. One, that she'd surrounded herself with the many stringed instruments in the room. And two, that she had to be the most earthly-looking woman I'd ever seen (with the possible exception, of course, of Maureen). In a pair of old jeans and a plain cotton work shirt, her straw-colored hair lightly streaked by the sun and her well-scrubbed face all flushed and freckled, she looked every bit the strapping young farm girl she was.

And that rustic image seemed even more fitting when she then plucked a sheet of song lyrics off of a music stand and began to fan herself with it, saying, "Gracious *me*, I can't think of the last time I had such a fright."

I was too brain-dead to come up with anything in the way of a reply, though, so I simply stood there nodding dumbly.

Which prompted Bonnie Jo to say, "What are you doin' here on a Sunday anyway? I thought you didn't work on the weekend."

"Normally I don't," I admitted. "It's just that I didn't have anything else to do today, so I thought I might as well come on out."

"Well if you're lookin' for somethin' to do," she told me, spreading her arms to indicate all the instruments at her feet, "you can help me to swap out these old strings. Ellie liked to replace them every now and again, so I thought maybe I'd try to keep that tradition alive for awhile as kind of a tribute to her."

"Did you guys play together?" I wondered.

"All the time," she said. "We were music buddies." She stopped to think that over. "And gardenin' buddies. And talkin' buddies. And basically just buddies in general. She was kinda like an older sister to me, or maybe a favorite aunt or something."

"Mr. Frazier tells me that she was close to your whole family."

She tilted her head and gave me a look I couldn't quite interpret. "You don't know the half of it," she said. And then, hesitantly. "How bout if I tell you a quick little story?"

"You go right on ahead."

"All right then," she told me. "I believe I will. You see, my family's been on the farm down backa here since my ancestors first claimed it as a homestead in the early 1800's. Round about 1950, though, my dad got real sick and the rains wouldn't quit, so between the medical bills and the flooded crops we had to take out a loan on the land, but had a tough time keepin' up with the payments. And that of course put us in danger of losin' everything to foreclosure."

She paused to stare down into her lap for a minute, and then peered back up at me as if the rest of the story should be obvious.

"So Miss Harper stepped in to help out," I volunteered. "Is that it?"

"After a fashion," she said. "The fact is, she just flat out bought the entire property, but with the understanding that nothin' was about to change. We were still free to live on it for as long as we pleased. Only now we wouldn't have to bear any of the financial burden. She promised to see to all that."

And before I could even comment on how incredibly generous a gesture that was, Bonnie Joe then slapped her thigh and said, "But this is no time to be so damn serious, so how 'bout if we honor Ellie with a song? I've heard your band play, and I kinda like your music, but with me and Ellie it was all about traditional country, and roots music, and even some good old Appalachian foot-stompers that came straight outta the holler."

"Such as what, for example?" I wondered.

And rather than simply telling me, Bonnie Jo broke into the opening lines of a classic old-timey tune, "Will the Circle be Unbroken," a song that I'd been belting out for as long as I could remember. And seeing that I absolutely *love* to sing harmony—for some lucky reason my voice blends well with others—when she came to the "by and by Lord" part I laid a series of vocal notes directly on top of hers.

And my heart damn near jumped out of my chest when our voices came together so perfectly that we created this amazing harmonic, a vibration so powerful that all the instruments surrounding us suddenly began to reverberate in unison, filling the room with an ethereal hum and bringing a huge (if somewhat sheepish) grin to Bonnie Jo Murphy's face.

☆ ☆ ☆

The phone was ringing as I let myself into my trailer that afternoon, and I damn near fell over a chair in my rush to get to it. "Hello."

"Oh good, you're home," Nicki said. "I've been trying to reach you all day."

"Well I've been trying to reach you too," I told her, thinking that she sounded a little bit tired, although I didn't really want to know why.

"I just wanted to apologize for not making it to your concert last night," she continued. "I thought maybe you might have been worried."

"I *was* worried," I confessed, my voice coming out with a lot more emotion than I'd intended. "Especially after I called when I got home and you didn't answer your phone."

"There's a really good reason for that, Andy," she said patiently. "I'm with mom and dad up in Columbus."

And hearing that came as such a tremendous relief that I felt as if I might possibly float up off the floor. It was a short-lived sensation, though—for out of nowhere Nicki started to cry.

"What's the matter?" I asked her.

"My dad's having heart problems. Mom called at dinnertime yesterday and told me that he'd been having chest pains, so she'd rushed him to the hospital and was waiting to see if he'd had a heart attack. So I basically just hung up the phone and got in the car. I didn't even think to get ahold of you or anything."

"Is he okay?" I wondered, suddenly feeling a little guilty about all the petty fears I'd been letting get to me.

"Pretty much. They kept him overnight for observation, but didn't find any major damage to his heart or anything. He does have some serious blockage in a couple of arteries, though, so they're putting him on some sort of medication and debating whether or not he should have surgery. Also, the doctor told him that the pain he'd suffered could very well have been stress-induced, so he was advised to spend a little less time at the office. But otherwise he's doing just fine. I do think that I should stay here for a few more days, though, just to help out. You know what a handful my father can be."

She let her voice trail off for a moment. And then, tentatively. "So why are you so angry, Andy?"

And you know, even though this may seem hard to believe, I'd kinda been expecting that question. Seriously. She'd always been able to see right through me.

Case in point: "It's Joseph, isn't it?"

And what choice did I have but to admit to that? Their relationship had been eating away at me all spring.

"Well I wish you'd please just *stop* it," she then told me. "Joseph and I are friends and that's *it*. We work really well together, and we're doing a lot of good for the Greek system on campus. But I don't have any feelings for him, Andy, and the sooner you get that through your thick head the better off we're going to be. Okay?"

And how did that make me feel? Oh, let's see. Maybe as if I was about the most stupid jackass ever to have walked this planet. "I am so sorry," I told her, not knowing what else to say.

"Well I'm sorry too, Andy. I'm sorry that you don't trust me, and I'm sorry that we haven't been getting along because of it. All this tension's been driving me crazy. So can we maybe just forget about Joseph for now, and simply get back to being *us*?"

"There's absolutely nothing I'd like better, "I told her.

And I once again felt as if I might float up off the floor when she answered quite sincerely, "Me either."

Chapter Ten

A cardinal sang out from the top of the oak tree I sat under in Ellen Harper's expansive side yard, while next to me Jonathan Frazier gazed down off the ridge and out into the valley below, his wicker lawn chair creaking softly as he leaned back to take a sip of mint julep. A little something, he'd just explained, to settle his nerves, for his flight that morning had been quite the adventure.

"Indeed," he then said, looking casual but elegant in a white linen suit and open-collared shirt. "I can't recall ever having been subjected to such severe turbulence before. At one point we must have dropped a hundred feet in a matter of seconds, and if that alone wasn't enough to upset me, the panic that then ensued among a few of my more excitable fellow passengers most certainly *was!*"

"I'm just glad you got down safely."

"As am I, young man," he told me. "As am I." Taking another sip of mint julep, he then turned to give me a smile, his trim grey mustache curling up at the edges and his eyes taking on a fatherly warmth. "And now," he began, "about Miss Harper. I somehow suspect that you'd like to hear more about her relationship with the New York literary world."

"I sure *would*," I admitted, "since what I've read in her new novel so far suggests that it wasn't just the fame and fortune she rebelled against. It was the whole *process* of becoming a successful author."

"That's very observant," Mr. Frazier told me with an appreciative nod. "She did indeed find the entire experience a terrible disappointment. For example, she was forced to endure lengthy and at times bitter battles with the editor first assigned to *The Sky's the Limit*, because he'd once made a failed attempt to become an author himself, and she felt that he therefore had his mind set on reshaping *her* work according to *his* point of view, simply to soothe his bruised and battered ego."

"And it seems to me that she didn't care much for the commercialization of her novel either, did she?"

"My heavens no. She was particularly upset with the cover art her publisher chose to use, because she felt that it was overly sensational, and would take away from her reputation as a serious writer."

Sighing as he thought back, he then set his mint julep on the arm of his chair and brushed a ladybug off his lapel. "But more than anything else, it was the constant barrage of reviews she abhorred. And to her way of thinking it didn't matter if they were positive, or negative, or even lukewarm. One way or another she simply refused to read them, for she believed that the more she focused on the highly subjective commentary of the critics, the more she'd be drawn away from her own true voice, and her own true vision, and both were, if I may be so bold as to say, absolutely sacred to her. And therefore she wanted to keep them as purely hers as was humanly possible."

And as a look of fond remembrance then came over Jonathan Frazier's face, I couldn't help but wonder about my own future as a writer, and whether or not I truly had what it took to someday develop such a high degree of dedication and determination. For if I *didn't*, then there was no way in hell that I could ever aspire to be a serious writer like Ellen Harper. And at that very moment the thought of having to live up to the lofty example she'd set weighed all too heavily upon my troubled young mind. All too heavily indeed.

✡ ✡ ✡

Having waited out a torrential early morning thunderstorm, I'd then wandered on down to Willow Creek and was sitting atop a massive rock that jutted out onto the swollen current, idly watching a piece of driftwood as it rushed downstream, around a bend, and ultimately out of sight. And as I then began to consider the long and tumultuous journey that lay ahead of it,

I found myself remembering the conversation I'd had with Jonathan Frazier the day before, and how it had set me to thinking about the literary journey that lay ahead of me. I was especially intrigued by what he'd said about Ellen Harper's devotion to both her voice and vision, for it made me wonder about how those concepts applied to the handful of stories I'd turned out so far. And the more I thought about it, the more I realized that it was far too early in my development as a writer for me to have found my voice—although I did have faith that if I kept on writing, and remained patient, it would eventually begin to emerge.

As for my vision, however . . . well, that was another matter altogether, for I was pretty sure that I'd already formed at least a vague idea of one. I wanted to carry on the work of the American Transcendentalists, who'd put so much of their creative energy into establishing a literary tradition for their newly emerging nation, a tradition based on the infinite promise of what was then considered to be the greatest social experiment of all time. And *oh* what high hopes they had too: Mankind living close to nature, developing spiritually, and learning to coexist in harmony, ideals they believed to be the very heartbeat of the new American culture.

And as the still-rising waters then began to lap up around my feet, it dawned on me that my own generation was at that very moment singing the praises of many of the same ideals. And that made me feel pretty damn lucky to be coming of age right then. Which, by the way, is exactly how Thoreau had felt back in the heady days of the mid-nineteenth century. In fact in some ways I even saw myself as kind of a modern day Henry David, tall and gangly and totally awed by the natural world—not to mention inspired to write by the spirit of hope pulsing so potently all around me.

Imagine that: *Of* my generation, but rooted in a literary history more than a hundred years old. What a *wonderful* position to suddenly realize I was in!

And what a *hell* of a lot of responsibility came right along with it.

✳ ✳ ✳

It was while poking around in Miss Harper's library later that afternoon that I made my next two important discoveries. As you may remember, I'd first come across the rough draft of her new novel buried in a stack of old letters beneath her desk, and ever since then I'd been curious about what made those old letters so precious to her that she'd felt the need to save them. I'd resisted the temptation to open them, though, because they were, after all, Miss Harper's personal property, and actually none of my business. On that day, however, I'd waffled a bit by convincing myself that there'd be no real harm in simply looking through them.

Not that I ever really got around to that, though, because no sooner had I picked up the top envelope and read what was written on the front—May 1946—than I noticed the corner of a leather folder sticking out from the bottom of the stack. Of course my initial reaction was that maybe I'd finally stumbled onto the rough draft of Miss Harper's *first* novel, *The Sky's the Limit*, and even though I was sorely disappointed when it turned out that I hadn't, it was an extremely valuable find nonetheless—because the folder contained all of her many notes on *Clouding Over.* And in spite of the fact that they proved to be almost as hard to read as the rough draft itself (each and every last one having been scratched out after use), I could still make out just enough of what they said to realize that I now had a reliable cross-reference to work with. And that was certainly enough to bring a smile to my face.

But it was the second discovery I made that afternoon that really set my heart a-pounding. There were two notecards tucked into the back of the leather folder, each of which contained more of Miss Harper's insights into the creative process. Unlike the ones I'd previously read, however, these hadn't been written in a highly objective second person voice. Rather they'd been written in the intimate first person, which in my eyes therefore made them just that much more revealing.

And I was even more pleased when I then found that each of the notes also fit quite nicely into one or the other of the two categories into which I'd organized Miss Harper's earlier insights. The notes on the first card were decidedly practical, whereas those on the second were decidedly profound. And since I don't think it would do either of them justice to merely paraphrase, here are what they said verbatim . . .

Card one:

I cannot overstate how important it is for me to write in longhand, for my handwriting offers a distinct reflection of who I am as a person, and I therefore want my words to emerge from the unknown in symbols that convey my own unique spirit, and not the generic spirit of the standardized symbols created by the pounding of typewriter keys.

It is also crucial for me to "hear" the words that I write, for it is not only their meanings I am drawn to, but also their melodies, and rhythms—their music as it were. Because a word without music has no power to persude. In fact the look and the sound of the language that flows through me are so deeply ingrained in my creative process that without the energy they contribute it is highly conceivable that I would no longer be able to write at all.

The look, the sound, and the meaning. It is impossible for me to separate any one from the others.

And card two:

Although it has taken me years upon years to finally get to this point, I now realize that ~ write in a semi-dreamstate devoid of both space and time. I'm neither aware of where I am, or if minutes or hours are passing. And I've also come to know that the true wonder of that dream-state is the ever mysterious force that lies behind it, the words eventually appearing on the page in a process as far out of my conscious control as the size and the shape of my cheekbones. And oh the joy it brings me to tap into the mystical powers of that ethereal presence! It makes me feel as if an infinite stream of light is forever pulsing through me. And at the moment I can think *of no greater blessing. I am a very fortunate woman indeed.*

Fortunate!? I'll say. I mean, she could actually *feel* the creative energy of the universe pulsing through her as she wrote! And as I then slipped the notecards back into the leather folder, my gaze drifted out through the bay window and on into the sky, and I found myself wondering if *I'd* ever become so deeply immersed in my work as to experience such a transcendent sensation. Or if, for that matter, I'd ever even be worthy of one.

☆ ☆ ☆

I don't know if you've ever been inside an armory before, but if not it's kinda like a gigantic basketball arena with all of the hoops and the seats removed . . . just a big old cold and drafty room with ceilings a good fifty or sixty feet high. And since the one I was standing in was where they held the local Armed Forces Physical Examination, there'd been various testing stations set up throughout. Of course I knew to expect that, because Ritchie Starkey had gone in for his physical a couple of months before, and he'd explained the entire ordeal in excruciating detail. So I was fully prepared to be weighed and measured, and to have my eyes and ears and testicles checked, and even to bend over naked alongside eleven other hapless souls while a military doctor walked down the line behind us, ever so intently shining a flashlight up our *butts!* (Although to this day I still have no idea just what it was he was looking to find there.) But what I *wasn't* prepared for—since Ritchie Starkey hadn't had to go through one—was the national security interrogation.

It came about like this. After finishing our physicals my group was led into a classroom of sorts, where we were told to fill out a Military Intelligence form that asked questions like, "Have you ever been a member of the SDS?" And,

"Do you associate with anyone in the Communist Party?" And so on. I mean, some of the questions were so downright ridiculous that it was all I could do to keep from laughing out loud.

But not the last one. It had a deadly serious effect on me, for what it asked was, "Have you ever been subjected to a security hearing, and if so why?" And since I of course had been—for my recent "draft card" speech at the university—I wrote "yes" and told my story, employing every literary technique I could think of to cast myself in a sympathetic light.

And yet for once my writing skills must have failed me, for within minutes after I'd submitted my form an MP showed up to order me out of my seat and march me down a narrow hallway to what couldn't have been a more clichéd interrogation room. In fact after the MP had left me sitting alone at the room's one tiny table, the blatantly obvious two-way mirror on the wall across from me reflecting the light of the single bare bulb that dangled overhead, I half-expected Sgt. Joe Friday of *Dragnet* fame to come striding through the door. ("Just the facts, Mr. Adamson. Just the facts.")

Although as usual that was only my imagination at work. The truth of the matter is that I sat there all by myself for what seemed like an impossibly long time before the door swung open and two crew-cut men in dark blue suits strolled in, identified themselves as FBI agents, and promptly sat down at the other side of the table. One was middle-aged, and the other surprisingly young, no more than his late twenties at most. And all things considered they were pretty damn friendly. In fact I didn't even really feel as if I was being interrogated at all. Or at least not at first. It was more like I was carrying on a casual conversation with two guys I'd just met in a bar. And in hindsight I suppose that had to have been a part of their strategy all along. I have to admit that it worked really well too. I was more than happy to spill my guts.

"So," the middle-aged man began, leaning his elbows on the table and giving me a grin. "You don't believe in the draft, huh?"

"No, sir. In all honesty I don't. But that doesn't mean I'm a radical or anything. After all, I didn't actually burn my draft card, you know. It was just a photocopy. And I only did it to fulfill a speech assignment anyway."

"Seems like it was pretty darn effective," he said with what I took to be an understanding nod.

"Yes, sir. It was. I ended up getting an 'A'."

At that point the younger man joined in, and his voice was just as genial. "So are you saying that if you were drafted you'd report for duty?"

"Most likely," I told him. "Although to be perfectly frank the whole idea's so foreign to me that I haven't even really given it all that much thought."

He merely smiled a little and sat back in his chair as if satisfied with that reply. The older guy, however, looked a little more skeptical, as if maybe he couldn't believe that I was truly that naive.

"Chances are you'll have to carry a gun," he said then. "Would you be willing to do that?"

And since that was the first time I'd ever even *considered* that possibility, I didn't have a clue as to what to say—which pretty much set the standard for the rest of the interrogation. In a tone that grew increasingly more serious by the minute, J. Edgar's boys peppered me with questions like," What do you think of the military involvement in Vietnam?" "If sent to defend your country would you engage the enemy?" And even, "Do you support the government's current stance on the anti-war movement?" And boy did that put me in a strange position . . . because each and every question stirred up so many conflicting emotions that even though I did my best, I wasn't able to give them any really straight answers. So by the time they were finally finished with me, both men were so thoroughly frustrated that they were on their feet, glaring down at me as if I'd just insulted their mothers or something. And then just like that they were gone.

And once again I sat there all by myself for what seemed like forever . . . until the door suddenly flew open and the younger man came barging back in to fingerprint me, take mugshots, and have me validate a transcript of the interrogation that had been typed up by some junior bureaucrat on the other side of the mirror. And then with a dismissive shake of his head, he looked down on me as if I was a pitiful excuse for a man and said, "We're recommending that you be given a 4-F, which in your case means morally unfit to serve." After which he spun on his heel and left for good.

And I was so dumbfounded that I couldn't even move. I mean, morally unfit to *serve*? That didn't make any sense at all. Because if I was morally unfit to serve, then by logical extension I was also morally unfit to go to war, and morally unfit to kill. And to this day the irony of being rejected for that's almost more than I can bear.

✵ ✵ ✵

I could hear Bonnie Joe rummaging around downstairs as I made yet another search of Miss Harper's library, hoping against hope to somehow finally come up with the rough draft of *The Sky's the Limit*. Or at least that was the plan anyway. She'd take the lower floor. I'd take the upper. And maybe, just maybe, one of us might get lucky.

At the moment, however, I'd become a little distracted. Encouraged by the fact that I'd already found two notebooks buried in among them, I'd decided to take one last look through the stack of old letters beneath Miss Harper's desk— although as fate would have it that wasn't to be. For I'd no sooner ducked under there than I had a weak moment and at long last succumbed to temptation. Removing the top envelope (the one dated May 1946), I carefully opened it and drew out the neatly creased sheet of stationary inside. And after then hesitating for a guilt-ridden second or two, I unfolded it and began to read. I have to confess that I didn't get very far, though, because the letter had been written in Miss Harper's hand, and it was so intensely personal that I was suddenly ashamed of myself for having so selfishly invaded her privacy:

The stories never read to you, the songs never sung. The blankets never tucked around your shoulders.

*These are the moments that are
lost to me forever . . .*

And that was all I could take before my shame overwhelmed me. Refolding the letter, I slipped it back into the envelope and returned it to its place at the top of the stack. And as I then fought back the self-disgust that began to well up within me, I was struck by the thought that the many rumors surrounding Miss Harper's seclusion had certainly been accurate in at least one vague respect. No matter who she'd written that letter to, or exactly what the circumstances might have been . . . she'd most definitely spent years harboring some really deep secret.

Not that I actually got much of a chance to pursue that train of thought, though—for right then Bonnie Jo came bounding up the stairs and into the middle of the room, excitedly waving an old leather folder back and forth over her head.

"*Got* it," she sang out as she saw me, her sunny farm girl smile as pure as the morning light that streamed in through the big bay window.

Chapter Eleven

"Splendid afternoon," Jonathan Frazier said, standing tall and drawing in a breath of the fresh country air, his right hand resting lightly atop the dapper walking stick at his side. We'd decided to get a little exercise by joining Bonnie Jo on a hike down through the forest behind Miss Harper's farmhouse to the lowermost of the three terraced gardens. It was fairly bursting with colorful wildflowers, and Bonnie Jo wanted to gather a few bouquets to brighten up the living room and kitchen. She certainly did look lovely too, in her earthy denim and gingham way, moving easily down the neatly planted rows, instinctively selecting what she felt were flowers of just the right color and texture. So entranced was I, in fact, that if Jonathan Frazier hadn't spoken up again I might have gone on gazing at her forever.

"So," he said. "You're about a third of the way through Miss Harper's new novel."

"Yes, sir. Having that other rough draft to work with really did the trick. But please keep in mind that we're only talking about a casual first reading. I haven't even begun to try to put together a formal manuscript or anything."

"In due time, my boy," he mused. "In due time. But as for the moment, would you say that you've learned anything of interest so far?"

I paused for a heartbeat as Bonnie Jo bent over to pick a handful of daisies. "Oh sure," I then told him. "I've learned quite a bit. But I guess what stands out the most is that she had to struggle so hard to be accepted by her peers. The popular belief is that everybody loved her, but if that novel's even close to being true to her real life, that wasn't the case at all."

"I'm sorry to have to admit that you're right," Jonathan Frazier said with a shake of his head. "Once she became a celebrity any number of people were quick to condemn her. I suppose that was only to be expected, though, because she was such a free spirit that her lifestyle often clashed with the social conventions of the day. Not only did she wear little or no makeup, for example, but she preferred pants to skirts, and had the audacity to tear around Manhattan in a dilapidated old pick-up truck. And since the more genteel among the literati found that to be abhorrent behavior in a woman, she was all too frequently subjected to both ridicule and scorn. Take me at my word, young man, it is never easy to rebel against the powers that be, and that was especially true for Miss Harper as a naïve young Appalachian girl in post-war New York City. Many are the times that she felt alienated and alone."

He broke off at that point and gazed out at Bonnie Jo, who was by now all the way down at the far end of the flower beds. Then he sighed heavily and looked back to me, his eyes full of the lingering sadness of some distant memory. "And of course her loneliness only intensified once she—"

And catching himself he broke off again, and I could tell from the tension along his jawline that he was struggling with whether or not to continue.

It was certainly a no-brainer as far as I was concerned, though. I mean, the suspense was damn near *killing* me! So I decided I'd better try to move things along just a bit. "Once she . . . *what?*" I wondered.

But it was too late. The sadness had faded from Jonathan Frazier's eyes, and he'd eased into a warm and gentle smile. "Just keep on reading, Mr. Adamson," he then said with a wink. "I'm sure there are many mysteries that have yet to be revealed."

And suddenly brandishing his walking stick as if it were a sword, he gave me a playful poke in the shoulder. "Many mysteries indeed."

✳ ✳ ✳

Invigorated by my hike back up through the forest, I'd just sat down at Miss Harper's desk when I inadvertently fell into an old habit: losing myself in my own reflection. Having heard a songbird I didn't recognize, I'd gone to look out the window and there I was, a faint image against a background of deep blue sky. And it was actually kind of fitting really, because ever since I'd found out that I was adopted my whole life had seemed oddly ethereal, as if I were indeed afloat in some vast expanse of space. In spite of doing really well in school at the time, and getting along with just about everybody, I'd simply never again felt as if I truly belonged. And because of that I'd always tended to keep to myself, spending hours upon hours alone in my room, reading, and writing, and listening to music, slowly developing what I now realize is an uncommonly fertile interior life. The key, it seems to me at the moment, to the religious conversion I underwent as I entered my early twenties.

It happened rather quickly too. I was raised Episcopal, confirmed at twelve, and eventually became so devoted to the Church that I served as an acolyte. And yet in spite my commitment there was always something missing. I mean, I read the *Bible*, and listened to the sermons, and took communion and everything. But for some reason there was nothing in either the doctrine or the ritual that touched me deep inside. In my *mind* I believed in what the Church was teaching, but in my *heart* I wasn't so sure. And there was a perfectly good reason for my uncertainty too, in that I was struggling with a feeling of spiritual isolation. There was simply no connection. No sense that I was a vital part of a greater whole, or that if I remained dedicated to my faith my soul would live on forever. In other words I felt every bit as alone in my spiritual life as I did out in the world at large.

But then as I went off to college I began to read the Transcendentalists, and it wasn't long at all before I found the inner peace my religious upbringing hadn't been able to provide. And strangely enough, it was a very simple message that made all the difference too. Don't look to the Church, the Transcendentalists said. Don't look to its Tenets and Laws. In fact, don't look to *any* outer source for your theology.

Rather turn your vision inward. Seek the truth within. We all have a Divine Inner Light, they said, the spiritual force that empowers all life. Look to the Light. Come to know the Light. That's where you'll find salvation.

And you know what? I already knew about that Light. I honestly did. In fact I'd known about it for as long as I can remember. It's just that until I read the Transcendentalists it had been nothing more than a gentle glow at the outer edges of my consciousness. And then *BOOM*, I learned of its spiritual nature and it came bursting forth within me, a brilliance so all-encompassing that it nearly brought me to my knees.

And now a few years later, in the summer of 67, that light continued to burn even brighter still. In fact as I came back into the moment I found myself looking straight through my reflection and on out into the endless sky, my entire being awash in the certainty that *everything* in existence is a vital part of the eternal Light, and that adopted or not, no matter how alone I still allowed myself to feel every now and again, on the deepest and most meaningful of all possible levels I would never really ever be alone at all.

Searching for something to do to pass the time until Bonnie Jo returned from Miss Harper's kitchen, I plucked a songbook off the music stand in front of me and casually began to leaf through it. It offered quite the selection too, a variety of tunes in different styles and from different musical eras—although what I was truly looking for was something really rootsy. You know, that good old mud-on-your-boots and pain-in-your-heart Americana soul. Bonnie Jo and I sounded so good singing together that I'd asked the band if she could sit in for a couple of songs sometime. And predictably, everybody was fine with that except for Michael. Prima donna that he was, *anything* that might upset the delicate balance of our performance agitated him no end. He was summarily outvoted, though, and therefore had no choice but to grudgingly agree.

So for the past couple of hours Bonnie Jo and I'd been trying out songs to see which ones fit our vocal style the best, and even though we'd already found two that we both really liked, I saw no reason why I shouldn't try to find a few more. The thing is, I had yet to come up with even a single one when a notecard fell out of the back of the songbook and fluttered down onto the floor. Picking it up, I instantly recognized Miss Harper's handwriting, and soon realized that it was yet another of her many creativity insights. The last I'd ever find, in fact, and by far the most profound.

The bedrock truth is, no one can tell you how to write, for there are as many ways of writing as there are people who put the pen to the page, or the fingers to the keyboard. And yet there is, however, a universal means of discovering how to write. You do so by writing. In other words the process is its own inspiration, and the more that you engage it, the more responsive it becomes. So if you want to be a writer, then write. Engage the process. For the more that you do, the more the process will develop a life of its own. And if in discovering how to write you delve deeply enough, you will one day transcend your own creative powers and tap into the infinite energy that gives birth to and sustains all of life as we know it. That is, you will tap into the ever-mysterious spiritual power at the heart of creation itself!

And looking up as I heard Bonnie Jo entering the room, I couldn't help but smile and shake my head in awe. "Miss Harper was certainly an amazing lady, wasn't she?"

Bonnie Jo gave me a quizzical look. "What makes you say that?" she asked, setting two cups of tea down onto the top of the little Fender amp beside her.

"Oh, just this note that I found in a songbook."

She glanced over at the card in my hand, a strand of straw-colored hair falling down across her cheek. "You inspired her to write it, you know," she then said.

"Pardon me?" I blurted, so startled that I was certain I must have misunderstood.

"You inspired her to write it," she repeated. "I was with her on the day that Mr. Frazier called to invite you out to the farm, and no sooner had he told her you'd be coming than a thought occurred to her and she scribbled it down and set it aside. I came across it as I was re-stringing the instruments last week, and not knowing what else to do with it I stuck it in her songbook. I never did take the time to read it, though. I just know that you inspired her to write it."

And with that in mind I felt an immediate need to look over the note again, and the words were so alive with Miss Harper's spirit that it was as if she were standing right there speaking them to me. I could actually see the sparkle in her bright blue eyes, and hear the Appalachian lilt in her voice. And even though it embarrassed the hell out of me to suffer such a weak moment in front of Bonnie Jo, I was suddenly overcome by such a deep sense of loss that out of nowhere I began to cry.

☆ ☆ ☆

"I missed you when you were gone, you know."

"I missed you too," Nicki said, turning her head to kiss the side of my neck. We were all snuggled up on my threadbare couch, kind of half-listening to the rain pouring down outside, just as we'd been doing for a good part of the time since she'd returned from Columbus a few days before. And I can't even begin to tell you how wonderful it felt to be getting along again. There'd been something really cathartic about our little spat over Joseph P. Wentworth III, and we were therefore indeed on our way back to just being us . . . exactly as Nicki had hoped. In fact I was feeling so good about our relationship that I didn't even mind that she was heading back up to Columbus the following afternoon.

"So how's your dad feeling about having to go into surgery?"

"About as good as anybody possible could, I suppose. He's sorry that the doctors have decided it's necessary, but you know what a realist he is. If it has to be, then it has to be. He just wants to get it over with."

"And when did you say it was?" I asked, drawing her in a little closer as a show of support.

"The day after tomorrow. And that's why I want to get home. I think it'll be good for him to have me there."

"I'm sure it'll be a big help to your mother too."

And as Nicki was just then nodding in agreement the phone in the kitchen began to ring. "Back in a minute," I told her, lifting my arm from around her shoulder and getting to my feet.

And oddly enough, it was my nearest neighbor on the line, a Mr. Robinson who owned the dairy farm a mile or so up Willow Creek. "Just in case you haven't heard," he told me, "the roads are beginning to flood. So if you need any supplies you better go out now, cause they're not countin' on this rain to quit anytime soon."

"Is the town cut off yet?" I asked him.

"Not at the moment, but I'm guessin' it will be. You were here back in 63, weren't you?"

I'll say I was, and I'd never seen anything like it. The entire valley flooded so bad that *all* of the main roads were underwater, and there was no way in or out except by boat. And if that alone wasn't shocking enough to a newly arrived eighteen year old, I then found out that the same thing had been happening every now again for the better part of the past century and a half. In fact so much time and money had been spent on repairing the damage over the years that the Army Corps of Engineers had actually been discussing the possibility of rerouting the river (which indeed they went on ahead to do in the mid-to-late 1970's).

But back to that pivotal phone call. "Well thanks, Mr. Robinson," I said. "I appreciate the heads up. Are you guys gonna be okay?"

"We're doing just fine here, Andy," he told me. "I've been through these floods before, you know."

"Yes, sir," I said. "I know that you have. Thanks again."

And hanging up I turned to Nicki, who having heard what I said was sitting bolt upright on the couch, a terribly anxious look in her eyes. "We've gotta get out of her *now*," I told her.

And so within minutes we'd gathered everything we needed and were ducking out into the rain. "Let's take my car," she suggested, angling towards the brand new Chevy Malibu convertible her father had recently bought her.

"We can't do that," I insisted. "We've got to take Betsy. I'll tell you why on the way."

And in spite of crinkling her nose at the mere thought, Nicki veered off in my direction and we slogged on across the yard, the water already spilling over the banks of Willow Creek and creeping up behind the trailer.

"Are you sure Betsy can make it?" she then asked as we climbed in.

"She'd better," I told her. "I spent a hell of a lot more than she's probably worth just to get her fixed last week."

And indeed, my faith in good old Betsy ended up paying off handsomely. In fact she proved to be much more than up to the challenge. Not only did she fire up on the very first try, but she purred along just as sweet as could be as we threaded our way through the rain-soaked hills. I was aiming for the state highway that ran northwest up to Columbus, hoping to reach the low spot near the river before it completely washed out— because once that stretch of road was impassable, nobody was going anywhere until the floodwaters receded.

Nicki was doing all that she could to bring us good luck too. Practicing Catholic that she was, she'd drawn a rosary out of her shoulder bag and was silently counting off the little white beads and reciting her daily devotions. And I don't mean to sound sacrilegious, but with her delicate features and porcelain skin she kinda reminded me of Audrey Hepburn in *A Nun's Story.* You know, what with constantly praying for God's blessing and all that. There was even this childlike innocence about her, a sort of a radiant purity I suppose I might say. And I'd be lying if I didn't admit that I'd never even noticed it before.

Unfortunately her prayers didn't really help a whole lot. As we rounded a wooded bend on our approach to the river, I could see that not only was the road already flooded out, but a car had been abandoned there with the water nearly up to its windows.

Pulling up as close to the waterline as I safely could, I then turned to Nicki, who was staring despondently out through the windshield. "Do you trust me?" I asked her.

And since the look she then gave me was totally blank I asked her once again.

"You know that I do," she said, obviously confused. "But why bring that up now?"

"Because I have to ask you to do something you're gonna be scared to do."

"And what's that?" she wondered.

"Do you remember when I told you about the last time this valley flooded?"

"Sure. It was your freshman year, but—"

I gently pressed a finger to her lips. "And do you also remember what I said I saw bobbing along on the water that covered the golf course?"

She thought back for a moment, and then her eyes went wide. *Real* wide. "You can't be suggesting . . ."

"Oh yes, I can. I'm suggesting just that. Volkswagen Beetles are watertight. They float. And that's why I said that we had to bring Betsy. If you want to see your dad before he goes into surgery, we have no choice but to push her across that washout."

"Do you *really* think that'll work?"

"I know damn well it will."

And after looking me straight in the eye for a good second or two, Nicki didn't even hesitate. "Let's go for it," she said.

So we scrambled out into the storm, and after making sure that all of the doors and the windows were closed, I told Nicki to grab a door handle and hold on tight. What we're gonna do is angle Betsy into the current," I explained, "so that way we'll hopefully drift over to where we want to be. Okay?"

And I've got to hand it to Nicki. In spite of the fear in her eyes, she gave me an immediate thumbs up. So I quickly reached in to shift Betsy into neutral, and off we went.

And you know what? Things couldn't have worked out any better. The water wasn't even yet quite waist deep, and the current wasn't really all that terribly strong. And if those two factors weren't blessing enough, Betsy was so buoyant as she floated along that she wasn't the least bit hard to handle.

So it couldn't have been more than a few minutes later that we were once again off down the road, soaking wet but almost giddy with a sense of accomplishment, two young lovers who'd just shared a grand adventure and were now feeling pretty damn proud of themselves.

And, I'd be remiss if I didn't confess, pretty damn proud of Betsy too!

✡ ✡ ✡

"So, Miss Harper got pregnant. Is that it?"

Jonathan Frazier looked up from the suitcase he was packing. In a navy blue sport coat and neatly creased khakis, he was dressed to catch an evening flight back to New York. "I rather wondered if she'd have the courage to write about that."

"I'll say she wrote about it. And she also wrote about the affair that led up to it, and about getting dumped, and about becoming so fed up with life in the city that she returned to southern Ohio. It's a really good book, Mr. Frazier, but I can see why she didn't write it when she was a lot younger. The story would've no doubt created a scandal, and maybe even ruined her career."

"You're absolutely right about that," he told me, laying in a final dress shirt, and then closing and snapping the lid. "And it would've ruined the life of her baby's father too. Which begs the question. Did the novel have much to say about him? And I ask because I was indeed aware that she was writing about their relationship, and seem to recall her debating whether or not it would be ethical for her to even go ahead and establish his identity."

"Well she never did," I said, folding my arms and leaning up against the doorway I stood in. "She did say that he was a highly respected family man, and quite a bit older than she was, but she referred to him only as 'Mr. Manhattan,' and gave us no real detail about his background whatsoever. Although she sure as hell didn't hold anything back when it came to their affair."

"He wasn't at all good to her, you know."

"That's what the story says. I mean, it's bad enough that he abandoned her after she became pregnant, but then to try to bully her into getting an abortion by threatening to destroy her if she *didn't?* Seriously. What kind of a bastard was this guy?"

He regarded me with kindly eyes. "In many ways he was actually a very good man, Andy, and for a time I believe he truly did have genuine feelings for Miss Harper. It's just that once she became pregnant, and he realized the devastating effects that would have on him both personally and professionally . . . well, let me just say that he became rather unsympathetic. And yet to Miss Harper's credit, she never did allow him to break her spirit."

"That comes out in the story too. But even though she held out against his selfish demands, she still blames all the psychological and emotional pressure she was under for the miscarriage she ended up having."

"The *what?*" Jonathan Frazier said.

And I was a little taken aback at how shocked he sounded. "The miscarriage," I repeated.

He just stood there staring at me blankly for a good long minute or two, and then shook his head thoughtfully and walked over to lay a hand on my shoulder. "There's someone far closer to the situation than me I believe you should be talking to."

✣ ✣ ✣

It was easily the most meaningful telephone conversation of my entire life. The "someone you should be talking to" was none other than the wife of Miss Harper's lover, who fittingly enough turned out to be her long-deceased publisher, the literary powerbroker Olaf Stevenson. And I'll forever be thankful to Mrs. Stevenson, because she couldn't have been any more helpful, or any more gracious either.

"It all just seems so very long ago now," she told me with a sigh, "that I simply see no reason not to discuss it anymore—although I must say that I feel the need to be completely honest with you, in that I don't know how much information I can actually provide. Yes, I knew about the affair. And yes, I told

Olaf that I would divorce him if he didn't end it. But I never did press him for any of the sordid details. That would have been far too painful for me."

"And he's been gone for how long now?" I asked her.

"He died in the fall of 1960, so it's been almost seven years. And I miss him to this very day, Mr. Adamson. I really, truly do. But one must move on. There's really no other choice. And so please tell me what it is that you would like to know. About all Jonathan said when he called to ask if I'd speak with you was that you were editing Ellen Harper's new novel."

"Exactly. And I'm just trying to clarify some of the finer points to make sure that I'm reading it correctly. I'm especially interested in finding out about the strain Miss Harper was under that led to her suffering a miscarriage."

There came a deep silence at the other end of the line. And then, "I'm sorry, but did you say a 'miscarriage'?"

"Yes ma'am."

"Very well then, I'm afraid there must be some mistake. Miss Harper didn't miscarry. She gave birth to a healthy baby boy whom she then gave up for adoption. In fact I'm rather surprised that Jonathan hasn't already made that clear to you."

"And why would you say that, Mrs. Stevenson?"

"Because, my dear boy, it was Jonathan's law firm that brokered the adoption."

And even though we must have gone on talking for another twenty minutes or more, I was so puzzled as to why Mr. Frazier hadn't simply gone ahead and told me about the baby himself that I can't for the life of me ever recall even a single other word she said.

Chapter Twelve

Part of the problem was the heat. I mean, even with all the windows open and the ceiling fans spinning like crazy, it was still downright sweltering inside *The Hayloft*—and that had the capacity crowd feeling more than just a little bit restless. Of course it didn't help any that we were in the midst of what's easily the most raucous and rowdy of all the songs I've ever written. It's a country music parody about life in Trailerpark USA called "She Turned to Jesus (and He Turned to Beer)." And it's a big-time fan favorite because the title's also the chorus, and everybody absolutely *loves* to sing along to it. Seriously. Just see if you can resist.

"So when their neighbors bought
that doublewide
they'd been coveting for years.
That's when . . .
She turned to Je-sus, a-and he
turned to beer."

Or,

"So when their high school daughter
came home to announce:
"I'm pregnant, again!' Oh dear.
That's when . . .
She turned to Je-sus, a-and he
turned to beer."

See what I mean? Anyway, the point is that we'd whipped the crowd into somewhat of a frenzy, and there was no question about the fact that the band was feeding off that energy. It was Ritchie's final night in concert before heading off to basic training, so he was really playing his heart out, pounding away on his drums as if his very life depended on it. And Maureen and Little John were still riding high on the exhilaration of her test results, so needless to say they were all pumped up.

But more than anyone else, it was Michael whose performance that night approached a fever pitch. Not only had he been drinking hard for the better part of the afternoon, but he was just sloppy enough that he'd confided in me as we took the stage that he'd gone "commando" under the tight jeans he wore to give himself an erotic rush. And because of that he was in truly rare form, working the crowd relentlessly, coming on strong to all the women, and in general playing his rock star role with more sex-crazed passion than I'd ever seen.

And then once again there was Julie. As always she hovered right in front of the stage, her slender body swaying seductively to the rhythm of my guitar. And yet much to my alarm, not only were her normally adoring eyes alive with a manic intensity, but as I looked closer I could see that she was holding a razor blade, and as soon as she saw me notice it she began to pantomime slitting her *wrists!*

You know what, though? At the risk of sounding heartless, she wasn't even my main concern. Not by a long shot. I was a hell of a lot more worried about Nicki. She was standing at the back of the crowd, visibly upset, and doing her best to simply hold her ground in all the chaos swirling around her. Even worse, I could see a drunken hillbilly slowly making his way up beside her. I'd run into him at the "feeding trough" urinal during the band's last break, and he'd launched into a spittle-filled tirade about my "prissy sorority girlfriend," and how she was so stuck up that she wouldn't even talk to him. And then he'd blabbered something about her sorority probably having a really stupid name like "I Felta Thigh," and stumbled on off to the bar.

And now here he was coming up on her. The timing couldn't have been any worse either, because Nicki was an absolute mess. Not only had her father's surgery taken an awful lot out of her, but earlier in the day she'd had a serious falling out with Joseph P. Wentworth III. He'd stopped by her dorm room to check on her right after she got back from Columbus, and in the midst of giving her a comforting hug he'd gone just a little too far. And when Nicki had then politely asked him to stop, he'd tried to physically force himself on her. The bastard. A good hard slap to his face had brought him back to his senses, though— after which Nicki had ushered him out of her room, and out of her dorm, and out of her life altogether.

So as I'm sure you can imagine, she was a little on edge, and when Mr. Drunken Yokel came sliding up beside her I just knew there was going to be trouble. And wouldn't you know it, as the entire roomful of sweaty fans jostled and jumped around, screaming out "She turned to Jesus" for all they were worth, that redneck reached over and grabbed her by the thigh.

And that's about all that I can recall. They tell me that I was down off the stage in a flash, fighting my way through the densely packed crowd and taking him to the floor with a clean, hard tackle. But all I remember is a white-hot explosion of anger, and then a flurry of flailing arms and legs . . . until I was suddenly being hauled up by the scruff of my neck to stare dumbly into Little John's deepset eyes.

"No fighting," he said.

And to show you how surreal the entire experience was for me, the only thought to cross my mind at that point was that I hoped he hadn't torn the Newport Folk Festival t-shirt I wore, because I'd bought it in 1965, the year Dylan had gone electric, and so of all the t-shirts I'd collected over the years it was far and away my *favorite*!

Nicki and I made love later that night, and unlike a few weeks earlier, when she'd just been going through the motions, this time she threw herself into it with total abandon. Never had I known her eyes to drift so far away, or for her body to be so responsive. And I have to admit that I did everything in my power to be the gentle and sensitive lover she needed then too, for I knew in my heart that she was seeking the inner peace that can only be found through a synergy of physical and emotional release. And as we moved back and forth between sudden bursts of unbridled passion and quiet interludes of tender touching, I could feel her slowly letting go. Out came her worries about her father. Out came her anger at Joseph P. Wentworth. And if I were to venture a truly daring guess, I'd say out came her fears about my need to be a writer (or at least for a little while anyway).

And then once we were both completely spent, and had nothing left to give, we curled up together on our sides like spoons and, the fallout from her failing to return to her dorm be damned, we slept peacefully until the sun rose high upon a brand new day.

It's kinda funny really, in that as I loped along the old Jeep road I'd worked out on practically everyday for the past couple of years, I suddenly developed a heightened sense of the Appalachian countryside I'd come to know so very well. I mean, the grass seemed greener, the flowers more colorful, and the song of Willow Creek more melodious than ever. And you know what? It wasn't just the elevated state of my relationship with Nicki that had me seeing my whole world anew either. It also had a lot to do with the dramatic conclusion to Miss Harper's new novel, in which Eleanor Taylor becomes so beaten down by life in the big city that she retreats to the comforting hills of her youth to seek solitude, and to heal. She simply no longer has the strength to deal with the ongoing aftershocks of her unplanned pregnancy, and doomed affair—not to mention the constant go-go-go of being a literary celebrity, what with all the interviews, and the readings, and the signings, and so on. She's just plain worn down to nothing.

So back she goes to southern Ohio, to the trees, and the streams, and the fields she loves. And that's where, as the seasons and the years slowly pass, she finally finds the peace she so desperately needs.

As, I must say, I'd found a similar peace on that lovely June morning. Yes indeed. The water flowing. A warm wind blowing. And the sun shining down just as bright as could be. I felt as I ran along Willow Creek that I could've gone on running forever.

✳ ✳ ✳

As soon as Jonathan Frazier got back from New York I drove straight out to Miss Harper's farmhouse, where I found him sitting in one of the Adirondack chairs on the screened-in back porch. And I'd been so anxious to talk to him for the past few days that I'm sorry to say that I was rather rude.

"So," I began without any preliminaries whatsoever. "Why didn't you just come on out and tell me that she actually had the baby?"

He set aside the legal documents he'd been studying and looked up at me over the top of his reading glasses. "What, no 'Good morning, Mr. Frazier'? No 'How was your trip?' Just straight to the point I see. Very well then, I didn't tell you because I'm afraid that I wasn't at liberty to do so."

And since I had no idea what he meant by that, I just stood there in the hope that maybe he'd continue—although he certainly didn't appear to be in any hurry to. Removing his glasses and laying them on the arm of the chair, he then slowly closed his eyes and pinched the bridge of his nose, obviously deep in thought. A really long moment passed. Followed by another. And then just as I was beginning to think that he must have had nothing more to say, he released what sounded like a sigh of resignation and turned to give me the smallest of smiles. "If you read through the letters beneath Miss Harper's desk," he then suggested, "they will no doubt tell you everything you are so curious to know."

And that was more than enough encouragement for me. Tearing out from the back porch and through the kitchen and living room, I bounded up the stairs to Miss Harper's library and ran straight across the floor to her desk. And after then reaching under it to grab the top envelope, I once again checked out the date on the front—May 1946—and then returned to reading the letter I'd first started a good nine or ten days before.

The stories never read to you, the songs never sung. The blankets never tucked around your shoulders. These are the moments that are lost to me forever on this your very first birthday

First *birthday!?* I wondered. And the unthinkable possibility that occurred to me then damn near knocked me senseless. I was quick to recover, though, and ducking back under Miss Harper's desk I pulled out the entire stack of letters and frantically began to look through them. They were dated May 1947, May

1948, May 1949, and so on . . . all the way up to May 1967, for a grand total of twenty-two. And with my fingers practically trembling, I stared down at that final envelope for a pulse-pounding second or so . . . and then I tore it open, drew out the sheet of stationary inside, and read the tender words that would change my life forever.

It is with a heart full of hope
that I look forward to finally meet
ing you, my dearly beloved son.

And that was all the farther I got before my hands started to shake, and my eyes were suddenly blinded by tears.

☆ ☆ ☆

"In her heart she *des*perately wanted to tell you," Jonathan Frazer explained. He was on his feet by then, staring out through the screen and down into the valley below. A quiet and oddly serene moment passed . . . and then he slowly turned my way. "But in the end she remained silent because she simply wasn't certain that she had the right to so suddenly thrust herself into your life. In other words she felt as if she might be intruding, and that caused her an enormous amount of guilt. So after many long days and nights of internal debate, she settled on a compromise. She would invite you out to her home, and if you accepted she would merely bide her time and let the situation unfold as it may. That is, she would leave it up to fate to determine the final outcome. And if I may interject a personal observation, I would say that there's little or no question that over time she would have most definitely opened up to you. But alas that was not to be."

And strangely enough, I responded to that revelation in a way that continues to shock me to this very day. ""So it wasn't my story after all," I said.

"Pardon me?"

"She didn't really ask me out here because of my story, like she told me she did. That was all just a lie to get me *out* here!"

"Not in the least," Jonathan Frazier assured me. "In fact your story played a pivotal role in her ultimate decision to see you." He paused for a moment to guage my reaction, and then laid a wrinkled hand on my arm and said, "Allow me to be blunt. Miss Harper knew that she was in failing health. And she also knew, obviously, that you had a birthday coming up. So when she read your story and was deeply touched, she realized that the time had come to at the very least introduce herself to you. But not before she swore me to secrecy, a vow that I solemnly promised to keep no matter how things eventually turned out. And that is why I wasn't at liberty to tell you that she'd had the baby. I'd given her my word that I would not interfere."

He paused once again to gauge my reaction, and then his eyes crinkled at the corners and he eased into a smile. "Of course I didn't feel as if that should prohibit me from giving you the occasional nudge in certain critical directions. Hence the phone call to Mrs. Stevenson, for example."

He broke into a really wide smile at that point, and it was then that I realized how truly relieved he was to finally be able to tell me the truth. "And since you're so concerned about the intrinsic worth of your story," he then continued, "there's something else I believe you should know. The fiction competition you won? It was a blind read. Miss Harper had no idea the story was yours until long after she'd selected it. And it was the fact that she'd found herself so instinctively attracted to your writing that was ultimately the catalyst behind her inviting you out here."

Imagine that. It was my work that had drawn my mother to me. And I was still trying to figure out what to make of that when Jonathan Frazier threw an arm around my shoulder and led me on over to the Adirondack chairs. "But enough of that for the moment," he said. "We have so much more to talk about. For instance, there are the multiple boxes of personal belongings Miss

Harper has left for you, old photographs and keepsakes and the like. And then of course," he added as we both sat down, "there's the matter of her will . . ."

And as he leaned over to pick up the legal documents he'd set aside what couldn't have been more than ten minutes before, I could feel myself slowly slipping away, away from the moment, away from the day, and away from the person I'd always been. Away, and away, and away I slipped . . . on out into the bright future of what would forever be a much more complete and contented me.

AFTERWORD

So there you have it. What an amazing summer of 67 it actually turned out to be—the Summer of Love, as it's so often known, a truly innocent time of great promise and hope. And I'm proud to say that I certainly fell under its spell, as I continue to fall under it to this very day. I've long been married to Nicki. We have three incredibly beautiful children. And yes, I have indeed become a writer . . . just not the one I set out to be all those many years ago.

I'd imagine an explanation is in order. You see, discovering the identity of my birth parents led me to some pretty serious soul-searching, and within months I'd dropped out of the band and moved into my newly inherited farmhouse to fulfill my dream of writing full time. And I have to admit that I was pretty damn productive too, churning out four novels over the next ten years—although at best they were only moderately well reviewed, and never did really find an audience. So when my publisher then ended up letting me go, it was kinda like the final blow, and I haven't written a single word of fiction since.

And yet I really have no reason to feel bad about that, and I'm being perfectly serious too . . . for with each passing year I've enjoyed a deeper and more intimate bond with my ever-faithful muse. And how could that possibly be, you may wonder? Well I'm about to tell you. No sooner had I dropped out of Willow Creek than they asked Bonnie Jo if she'd take my place, and it quickly became apparent that she and Michael made musical magic together. So it wasn't long at all before the band landed a record deal and began to shoot straight up the charts, eventually becoming such a worldwide phenomenon that twelve Grammys and millions of album sales later they're still going strong. And that means that I'm doing really well too, due to the simple fact that I continue to write all their *songs!*

So I guess old Jiminy Cricket was right: Dreams really do come true. Or at least some of them do, even if they take on the most unusual forms, and sneak up on you in the strangest ways. Not that I'm complaining, mind you. Far from it. In fact I couldn't imagine being any happier than I am at this very moment. Along with my wonderful family life, and long and successful songwriting career, it just so happens to be one of those unbelievably beautiful late May mornings—and my birthday if the truth be told. So I think maybe I'll just wind up my work for the day, go for a run, and then take good ol' Betsy out for a drive. Yep, that's right. I said good ol' Betsy. Not only have I held on to her for all this time, but just this past winter I had her completely restored. And even though I'm extremely cautious about the weather I take her out in, on a day as lovely as today I simply can't resist.

Made in the USA
Charleston, SC
30 May 2014